WE ARE
NOT ALONE

WE ARE NOT ALONE

KATRYN BURY

HARPER
An Imprint of HarperCollinsPublishers

Library of Congress Control Number: 2023948571

ISBN 978-0-06-333741-1

Typography by Andrea Vandergrift

24 25 26 27 28 LBC 5 4 3 2 1

First Edition

* *

For Dr. Stuntz and Dr. Feehan,
without whom this story may never have been told

CHAPTER
* 1 *

On the morning of my first day of eighth grade, I find myself thinking about how spectacularly my cells have let me down.

Sure, they're small—as in the smallest living thing. But they have a population in the trillions. Our cells make up everything in our bodies, so it's pretty much a full battalion floating around in there. Strength in numbers.

And, yeah, I'm going to say it. They had one job— to be *chill*.

But what did they do? They went ahead and started multiplying their most unqualified loser cells instead of the ones that actually worked. The *opposite* of chill.

I'll bet most kids don't wake up thinking about this stuff. Our cells are one of those things in life we're supposed to count on. Like the sun rising and setting, and the ground under our feet. Like our heart beating, or how we wake up every day breathing air. It's a given.

But what if one day the sun didn't rise? What if the floor fell out from under us and became a giant abyss? Once my cells went rogue and became cancer cells, everything had a question mark.

Every morning, I take a breath to remind myself I can. I pause before I touch my feet to the floor. I check out the window to make sure there's still a sun, and I put my hand up to my chest to feel it beating. For a long time, it seemed like it couldn't get worse than that. This was bad, I told myself, but survivable. I could do this every day—if I needed to.

I thought that all the way up until the day my best friend Oscar's cells let him down for the last time.

"Hey, Cricket," Mom says gently, climbing into the driver's seat next to me. She tucks a frizzy strand of hair behind her ear and looks around the garage. "Are you really waiting for me in the car by yourself?"

"Are *you* really calling me by my baby name?" I force a smirk. She kind of cut into my thinking time, but maybe that's a good thing.

Mom feigns a thoughtful face. "Hmmmm. You're

saying Auddy and I shouldn't call you 'Baby Cricket' at school. Or, wait, maybe we should lean in! Cross out the name 'Sam Kepler Greyson' on every school form and write 'Baby Boy Cricket' instead."

I roll my eyes, but I can't help but smile for real that time. My moms are such dorks. They're always joking about how, when Auddy went with Mom to the first sonogram, I looked more like an insect than a baby. Which would have been awesome, now that I think about it.

Mom reaches for her seat belt and I reach for my morning toaster pastry.

"Are you ready for school?" she asks.

I point to my backpack and shrug as if to say *Ready as I'll ever be*, but that's not what she's talking about. "Is this about Saturday?" I ask.

Mom is blunt, as always. "Yeah, it's about Saturday. And about this being your first day at school since the end of January."

"Ah."

Mom lets out a breath. "Sam. You can't expect me not to ask if you're okay. You missed almost half a year and then . . . after everything that happened with Oscar, you're starting school a week late. It would be a lot for anyone. So, *are* you? Okay, I mean?"

I squeeze my eyes shut, hoping it will make her question disappear. It doesn't work, and a heaviness settles on my chest.

For a second, I imagine that I'm James Baskerville from my favorite show, *Otherworld*. If he can be strong enough to hold the portal closed to ward off thousands of interplanetary monsters, I can calm down for two minutes. Right?

"I'm feeling fine," I lie.

It's something I've done every day since my friend died. And a good part of the last year.

The thing is, I don't *like* lying. But it's . . . less complicated. The truth leads to a thousand more questions. And hospital visits. And crying. I know that telling the truth didn't, like, *give* me cancer. But sometimes it feels like it did. Like some twisted board game where every truth is a number on a set of dice, forcing us to move further down a path toward—

"I have a cough." *Move two spaces to see a doctor.*

"I took my medicine but the cough isn't going away." *Move five spaces, get an X-ray.*

"Yes, there is a missed call from the medical center." *Move one space, call back, then draw a card. Too bad—the card is a terrifying diagnosis!*

Sometimes it feels like "I'm fine" is more than a lie.

4

It's actually a giant force field, keeping out everything that comes after you admit that you're *not* fine.

"Oscar's service was beautiful," Mom presses when I don't elaborate.

"Not like he was there to see it," I point out darkly, shoving my mouth full of pastry.

"You never know," she replies softly. "Look, I know how hard that must have been for you after everything you've been through with your own diagnosis. But you beat it, kid. You're a survivor now. More than that— you're basically a superhero."

I snort. "Yep, that's me. A real warrior."

"Sam . . ."

"Come on, Mom," I go on with a humorless laugh. "The only 'battle' I remember is napping and eating lots of jars of peanut butter."

I bite my tongue before I can say what I think next: *If cancer was a villain to defeat, then Oscar would still be here. And I wouldn't be completely alone.*

"Actually, you're right," I say before she can reply. "I *am* a hero. Just like in that book, Percy Jackson versus *cancer*." I wiggle my fingers spookily so Mom will laugh like she always does, but she doesn't laugh.

She sighs.

"It's okay to say this scared you, Sam. You know that,

right? What happened with Oscar . . . it's even more complicated for you."

Usually making Mom laugh makes me feel better, so the fact that I can't hits hard. The big, impossible "Are you okay?" question weighs me down—so far that I worry I might disappear.

"Oscar had brain cancer, I have Hodgkin's lymphoma. It's not the same," I say with the flattest voice I can manage. "I wasn't scared, okay?"

Another lie. They multiply fast, but I can't seem to find a way around them—especially since I have two monumentally Big Things™ (that's right, I'm trademarking it) to deal with. I'm in cancer remission—Big Thing #1. And my best friend died from a different cancer—Big Thing #2. How is anyone supposed to treat you like a normal person after that? How are you supposed to *feel* normal?

"Okay. I get it," Mom says. "We don't have to talk about it until you're ready. I do want to ask something, though." Mom pauses, and I nod for her to go ahead. "I saw Mr. and Mrs. Padilla give you a book after the memorial. Was it Oscar's?"

Instinctively, I throw a glance at my backpack, thinking about Oscar and me, sitting in his bedroom and writing in our alien research book. The two of us had been researching unidentified aerial phenomena (what most call UFOs) for months. We were obsessed—but the kind of obsessed that feels good. Like a full stomach after your favorite meal.

Of course, picturing him triggers more memories— the worst ones from Oscar's last few days. The images come courtesy of that mean part of my brain. You know—the part that says you look ugly when you get a zit, or that you're a total failure if you get a bad grade. When you're dealing with Big Things™, it only gets louder.

Oscar and I had decided to name that part "Dr. Wrongbrain" for two reasons. One, because it reminded us of an old-timey villain. And two, using a name helped us shut him down. I desperately need to get rid of him now, but I don't think the name alone is going to cut it.

Squeezing my eyes shut, I force myself to visualize Oscar in his room. It's something I've been trying out lately—imagining us having a conversation like nothing happened. I always feel silly afterward, like I'm trying to conduct a séance. Still, I can almost hear him teasing me.

Hey, Broody McSadboy, I imagine him saying. *Stop torturing yourself.*

I laugh out loud at the image, only stopping when I see Mom's expression.

"Sam?" Mom says, a crease between her brows and a question on her face.

Oh, right. She's asking about our alien book. And probably wondering why I'm randomly cackling after she asked about my best friend's funeral. Wow. Can't explain any of that. Time to backtrack, Sam.

"It's nothing," I tell her. "Oscar and I made this book together about UFO sightings. That's why I laughed—I remembered us messing around and writing in it." I don't tell her the real reason because I don't want her face to go from regular worried to the one that screams *I need to talk to Auddy about this*. I definitely don't tell her about the other thing—the message Oscar left for me on the last page of the book that I can't get out of my head.

"I swear, it's *nothing*," I repeat, leaning back to show her that I'm the King of Casual.

Mom occasionally knows when to quit, so she doesn't push. Instead, she starts the car. Mom usually puts on a podcast, so I'm surprised when I hear a few ominous and melodic bars sound from the speakers. It's from the *Otherworld* movie soundtrack—the one from over a decade ago. A few minutes later, I hear Nina Simone—my all-time favorite singer—belting out "I Think It's Going to Rain Today."

"Did you make an all-Sam playlist?" I ask as the Nina song ends.

"Maybe." When the Perry the Platypus theme from *Phineas and Ferb* comes on next, she follows that up with a laugh. "Okay, yes."

A smile heats up my cheeks. We listen for a while until Mom pulls into the loading zone in front of Northborough Junior High.

I blink. School looks bigger somehow. Did it get bigger?

"Should I walk you in?" Mom asks nervously.

I side-eye her. "No, because I'm thirteen, not five. I'm a big boy now, remember?"

Mom laughs, and I mentally check that box for today. "Okay. Are you sure?"

I grip my backpack tightly. "Yes. I'm all good, Mom. *Really.*" Because apparently I need to punctuate my lies now.

Keeping my eyes trained ahead, I wave behind me after I close the car door. Then, I stalk through the front doors, ignoring the blaring voices around me and trying not to look like this moment is completely overwhelming.

I hear a "Hey, Sam" floating out from the crowd.

9

For a brief moment I wonder if that might be for me, but I shake it off. There are three other Sams at North-borough.

Unless it's Kevin. But, no. Of course it wouldn't be Kevin.

Anyhow, I don't have time for ex-friends. I need to look at Oscar's message again. Even though I've stared at it a thousand times, I feel like I'm missing something. Once I make my way through the crowd, I can find a place to be alone and check it out again.

Taking a deep breath, I walk down the hall. One girl with glossy black hair glances at me, her eyes lighting up with recognition when she passes. For a second, I think she might say something. Instead, her expression withers into something like disgust. I catch a similar nervous look from a tall guy I remember from my pre-algebra class last fall. What the heck?

Maybe they heard I was sick and they don't know what to say. Whatever.

I duck into a bathroom stall, huddling next to the lock. As soon as I'm sure nobody's coming, I reach for my backpack and pull out the book.

It's leather-bound, because of course it is. Oscar was always a fancy-journal guy. The front page has a sketch of an alien welcoming us to their home world and a scrawled title that reads: *Oscar and Sam's Guide to Finding Intelligent Life.*

Skipping all the notes we'd done together, I flip to the last page—the one I can't stop thinking about. My breath steadies and my shoulders relax as I stare down, running my fingers over a crudely sketched symbol that accompanies Oscar's last words to me:

We've got to keep looking, Sam. We are NOT alone in the universe.

CHAPTER
* 2 *

I realize it's not fair to throw shade on someone who died. Especially someone as awesome as Oscar. The guy is . . .

(was)

. . . my best friend.

That being said, dude could have been more specific. *How* are we not alone in the universe? What does this symbol mean?

As I sit down in social studies at the end of the day, I find myself scrolling past all the articles we'd found together on my phone and hoping one of them has a clue as to what he meant. If I'm going to figure out what Oscar was trying to say before he went and died on me, I'm gonna need more.

More students file in, but I try to ignore the noise and focus.

"No, no, man. After school!"

I flinch, looking up as I recognize the last voice I wanted to hear.

Freaking. *Kevin.*

He wasn't in any of my earlier classes. I even ate in the library today to see if I'd be lucky enough to make it through a whole day without seeing him. Looks like my luck ran out.

My body rigid, I lowkey watch him pass me and sit in a chair near the front. Wow. He got way taller. Not that I care.

Once I'm sure his back is to me, I go back to swiping through UFO articles on my phone. Head down, Sam. *No contact.*

"Phones away, please!" Ms. Wong says loudly as she passes my desk. "You know better."

I mumble an apology and stuff my cell into my backpack, but the damage is already done. Kevin turns, staring right at me. Then, he glances at Ayden Fu in the next row. Both of them exchange an amused look.

Fantastic. Although, at least it's one weird look I *expected* today.

I'm sure Kevin told everyone about the cancer by now, and that we're decidedly not friends. We *were* friends— since the first day at Northborough Junior High last year. But he hasn't spoken to me since February. It's probably for the best that Kevin never knew about Oscar. He'd do more than look at me funny. He'd probably tell everyone I was cursed.

I feel cursed.

"Hey, thanks. You saved me from getting yelled at about *my* phone," a whisper cuts through my self-pitying thoughts.

I blink at this girl, Rose, in the row next to me. I remember her from last year—she's nice. A little weird, which is a compliment. I'm pretty sure she has a Marvel obsession, based on the sheer number of Thor and She-Hulk sketches I see in her notebooks. She's also the only one who hasn't looked at me like I have two heads today.

Annoyingly, when I try to smile at Rose, I find myself blushing head to toe. "Um . . . you're welcome," I grunt like a total jerk.

Rose's mouth turns downward, and then she looks back up to the front.

Awesome, Sam. You *win* at talking to people.

That's one thing I forgot while I was home for the

bulk of the past eight months—the fact that talking to girl-type people makes me lose all ability to function. It's a preexisting condition I've had since fifth grade. Or maybe it's not a condition. Maybe I'm possessed, like the episode of *Otherworld* when this parasite creature, Gondii, made James Baskerville change personalities.

It's hard to explain the awesomeness of *Otherworld*, even though it's my favorite show of all time. Agent Baskerville is this world-renowned UFOlogist, and MI-6 asks him to look into a series of paranormal incidents. They pair him with one of their intelligence officers, Gemma Monroe, and most of the show is about them investigating paranormal activity. Mom introduced me to *Otherworld* four years ago and I've been obsessed ever since.

Yeah, and I admit it. Gemma Monroe is a big part of my obsession.

In part because I'm hetero and, come on, who *wouldn't* love her? There's nobody like Gemma. She may not be flashy, but she's so smart. And funny. For example, she's supposed to be this professional government officer, but she makes the silliest faces sometimes. And her hair. Sweet holy heck, that hair. It's red, and somehow looks both glossy and super soft.

I need a Gemma Monroe.

Of course, that will never happen if I keep malfunctioning around girls. Sigh.

Absently, I take my metallic gel pen to the top of my backpack and sketch the symbol Oscar had drawn in our alien book. When I'm done, I sit back and stare at the messy oval with three lines coming down. It looks exactly like a spaceship, with the lines as beams of light. But what are those jagged lines at the bottom supposed to be?

When Ms. Wong takes a phone call, the classroom gets loud again. I'm about to hide behind the sleeves of my hoodie when I stop. Everyone's words are crashing together, buzzing, but one familiar word breaks out from the pack:

Cancer.

Oh, man. Are people really talking about me while I'm right here? And what is it about cancer that makes people whisper it like it's a swear word?

Peering over my arm, I catch sight of my old academic nemesis, Leslie Choi-Blankenship. She's stink-eyeing me, along with Zooey Villapando and Cat Pellegrini. Seriously, what is going *on* with people today?

Last year, I admit Leslie and I got competitive after Principal Romero told us we were both in the running for this national debate contest. Both of us upped our game pretty hard and I wouldn't say we liked each other. But I've been out of debate club since last year, and I'm nobody's competition now. Why are Leslie and her friends glaring at me?

I shift uncomfortably in my chair, looking away from them.

"Today is the day!" Ms. Wong announces a moment later, putting the loud hum of class to rest. "It's time for the annual history project!"

Whoa, okay. Guess I came back to school on the right day. The California History Project is the biggest report in eighth grade. Kids partner off and study a major event from our state's history. There's a competition when we finish, and the winners get to do a special presentation in San Francisco. Mom and Auddy would probably show up with foam fingers, so . . . embarrassing. But it could boost my grades, which I really need after this year.

"We're going to do things a little differently this time," Ms. Wong is saying, holding out a plastic bowl with small folded papers inside. "When I come to your desk, please draw a slip."

That's weird. I heard that kids partner up for the California History Project. A sense of dread hits my gut. Is

Ms. Wong making it random? The dread creeps upward and becomes a full-blown panic. It could be . . . anyone.

I might get stuck with someone like Nathan Briones. All through sixth and seventh grade, he's been saying "Sam Kepler Greyson is so *burgundy*" when I'm within earshot, and then laughing with his friends. I think it's supposed to be an insult, but I don't get it. It's literally just a color.

Suddenly, I feel the heat of someone's stare on me from the front of class. When I glance up, I see Cat Pellegrini, of the Leslie Choi-Blankenship crew. Yikes. None of them would be awesome, either. When Cat spots me looking back at her, she immediately spins her head to the front. Then she flips her hair and leans forward to whisper to Leslie and Zooey. I see all three glance back at me pointedly.

I look away from them, and then dare to let my glance slip over to the worst possible scenario. What *would* happen if I got paired with Kevin? Would he spend weeks refusing to look at or speak to me while we tried to do the project? A wave of nausea comes over me for the first time in months, and bile gurgles at the back of my throat. I swallow and it feels like fire.

"Sam?" I look up to see Ms. Wong tucking her green hair behind her ear with one hand and extending a plastic bowl with the other. "Pick a number, okay?"

Clenching my teeth a bit too hard, I reach into the pile of jumbled papers.

"Twelve," I tell her, holding up the number.

"Okay!" she says, moving forward to hand a number to the next student.

One by one, I watch people draw numbers. Leslie high-fives Wei Li as they compare papers. Phew. Okay. No Leslie. Then, Ms. Wong hands a number to Kevin. After one agonizingly long moment, I see Kevin nod at Nathan Briones.

"Eight?" Kevin grunts.

"Eight," Nathan grunts in reply.

I let out a relieved breath. Two birds, one number. Although . . .

Wait.

Ms. Wong is gesturing to Cat Pellegrini, who holds a matching quarter sheet of paper that reads—you guessed it—twelve.

My stomach drops, but I immediately try to find a bright side like Auddy would. Because this won't be *so* bad. I've barely talked to Cat, and it's not like she can hold the Leslie thing against me so badly that we can't finish a project. Right?

"All right, that's it!" Ms. Wong says, placing the empty

plastic bowl on her desk and picking up a second one. "Now, go sit with your partners and we'll draw subjects."

Cat stands to face me, her face frozen in an almost theatrical cringe, as if Ms. Wong is forcing her to do a project with a sewer rat. Everyone moves around, humming in conversation, but it seems to take her approximately one million years to reach my desk.

Once again, I find myself asking: What is *happening?* I wouldn't call myself "popular" last year, but it was nothing like this.

Someone to my left tosses a sloppily folded piece of paper, hissing, "Hey, Cat!" but the paper bounces off of the desk in front of me and floats, half unfolded, under my chair.

I reach down to get it for her, but Cat shouts, "Wait, that's for me."

"I know, I was just . . ."

I glance down to refold the paper and hand it to her but the top line is visible and I stop short. What I read actually makes my heart stop.

Do you think he really lied about having
CANCER?

CHAPTER
✶ 3 ✶

The words are like roots.

Each one pulls me down further into my spot, immovable. My heartbeat races so fast that it sounds deafening in my own head. It even drones out Dr. Wrong-brain, who usually loves to show up at times like this.

For a long beat, I consider my options.

I could stand up defiantly and ask who's spreading the lie. It would be epic. I'd show everyone the chemo port scar on my chest that looks like a sad worm, or the tiny blue tattooed dots I got for radiation therapy.

Or, I could simply go up and show Ms. Wong the paper. Quieter. Probably the smartest move. All my teachers likely know about the cancer, since Mom and Auddy have been in contact with the school the whole time. I was only in independent study so long because

Auddy was worried about there being another Covid surge while my immune system was shot from chemo.

I could go with either option. But, for some reason, I don't. Instead, I quietly fold the note and hand it to Cat like I never saw what was written there. She blinks at me for a moment, glances at the paper and then—eyes wide—shoves it into her pocket and flushes pink.

Wow. Well done, Sam. In one moment, I've tanked all my options. Because, now, Cat has the paper. If I wanted to tell Ms. Wong, she would have only my word to go on.

What does Auddy say? *Always document.*

"So," Cat says shakily. "I guess we're partners."

I can't seem to form words to reply. Am I in shock?

Do something, Sam! You're supposed to be some kind of disease-battling paladin. Percy Jackson versus this situation. Come ON!

"I guess so." The moment the words come out, I realize I'm not shocked at all. I'm angry. Furious, in fact.

Avoiding Cat's eyes, I stare at the front of the classroom. Wei Li, Leslie's partner, is holding their breath and drawing a subject. They roll their eyes and show Leslie. "California missions?"

My indignant heart soars with delight. Good luck trying to put a fun spin on the horrors of colonialism, *Leslie.*

"Can I pick next?" Cat asks, sounding bizarrely eager, considering her reaction to being stuck with me. "We're really excited."

I'm sorry, *what*?

Ms. Wong laughs. "Fine, Cat. Go ahead."

Cat hunches over the bowl, totally boxing me out, but whatever. I don't even care what we draw at this point.

"The 1989 Loma Prieta earthquake!" Cat calls excitedly.

Big Things™, twentieth-century style. Fantastic.

"Oh!" says Ms. Wong. "That's a good one."

Barely managing a thumbs-up, I hide my head in my folded arms on the desk. It blocks out Cat and Ms. Wong, but it doesn't stop me from obsessing. I don't understand. Who would say that I lied? And why? It's such a bizarre thing to make up out of nowhere.

"Hey," Cat says.

And why wouldn't Kevin correct people? Even if he's pretending I don't exist, he knows I was sick. . . .

"Hey!" Cat is snapping in front of my face.

"Huh?" I murmur.

Oh yeah, the project.

Slowly, I drag my eyes back to face her. I can figure this out later. I just need to get through the next fifteen minutes. Then I can go home and tell Mom and Auddy. After that, it won't matter that I gave the paper back, because they'll believe me.

"Sorry," I tell her evenly. "Just distracted. You know?"

She goes as stiff as one of my action figures, clearly understanding my meaning. "Yeah. Um, so anyway. Loma Prieta is a good topic."

"It's not a garbage topic," I concede through gritted teeth.

She rolls her eyes. "'Not garbage.' What a ringing endorsement." Then, Cat seems to notice my expression and softens. "Um, sorry. It's just that I'm psyched we got this one. My mom was here during the earthquake, so we have primary sources." I raise an eyebrow, and she repeats, "*Primary* sources."

"Sure," I say slowly, latching on to Cat's words for the first time since I saw that note. I did *not* expect her to fangirl out about primary sources. But, okay. "Anyway, we should settle on a work schedule. Should we meet at your house?"

Cat looks like she's considering it. "I need to ask my parents first. Maybe we could start here at school?"

"I think you need permission to do that if it's after school," I point out. "What about the Rose Garden Library?"

24

"The Rose Garden Library is fine," Cat chirps. "Let's start today at three-thirty? I have cheer practice some days, so we'll have to stagger the schedule." She flips through her notebook and writes down *Rose Garden Library*. Zoning out on her neat cursive handwriting, I notice something odd.

"Wait," I say, putting my hand on her notebook. "Do you already have a bazillion notes on the Loma Prieta earthquake?"

"No!"

"Then why does your notebook literally say 'Earthquake Facts'? You have, like, forty pages in your tiny little handwriting."

She puts a protective hand over her notebook. "It's not that tiny!"

Crossing my arms over my chest, I ask, "If we only drew the topic now, why would you have notes?" I'm not usually so confrontational, but this day is doing something to me.

Cat reddens, sputtering half explanations. "I don't . . . I mean . . . I never . . ."

"You're turning red," I point out. "Wait. Did you *cheat* to get this assignment?"

She gives me the world's most withering glare. "*Some* people are prepared. See you after school." Cat stands, pushing her chair back with a flourish.

Well, I guess I'm not getting that note. Whatever. The note wouldn't prove who started the rumor. It sounded like the note writer had heard it secondhand. My eyes follow as Cat flips her hair and stalks back toward her desk just as the bell rings.

Then, as Leslie, Zooey, and Cat group together, everything becomes crystal clear. I see none other than Kevin Bellman (former friend, current jerk) walk over. He grabs Leslie's hand, weaving his fingers with hers, and casts a very obvious look in my direction. Then he whispers something to Leslie, who shakes her head angrily. Cat and Zooey trade an uncomfortable look.

Oh.

I don't know why it didn't occur to me right away. Kevin was literally the only one at school I told about the cancer. This was my first day back at school. Who else *could* have started the rumor other than him?

My face hot, I grab my bag. Then, head down, I move past all four of them and imagine my cells multiplying so fast they become a swarm that sweeps me away for good.

CHAPTER
✶ 4 ✶

I walk up to the Rose Garden Library, storm away, and walk back at least five times.

I'm supposed to meet Cat, but every ounce of me is torn. Do I bail, and go home to tell my moms about the note right away? They always told me to go straight to them if I was being bullied. But . . . is this bullying? It's such a bizarro situation that I can't tell.

After fifteen minutes of obsessing (and fantasizing a million different nuclear-option ways I could confront Kevin) I decide to go inside. I already sent Mom and Auddy a text telling them I don't need to be picked up so that I could come all the way over here. If nothing else, maybe I can get more information from Cat to bring to them later.

I don't see her anywhere when I get to the library

study area, so I immediately shrug off my backpack and sit in one of the chairs at the end of the stacks. Of course, then I realize I'm sitting all stiff and upright like a dork. I need to calm down. Reaching into my bag, I take out my best chill pill—a time-worn paperback I always keep in my backpack. Flipping to a dog-eared chapter, I take turns reading and staring at the door.

Oscar used to say that books made him feel safe when almost nothing else did, because if you're ever nervous, you can flip forward in a book and find out what happens next. You can see that a happy ending is coming, or prepare for something bad.

The only problem is that I wish life followed the same rules. If I could have flipped forward in the pages of this year, I would have known what was coming when the doctor called us in January, haltingly warning that the news "wasn't good." I would have been able to keep myself from the shock when Mom and Auddy got the call about Oscar.

If that worked, I could flip forward and read the last page of my cancer story. I hope it's not a sad ending. I hope I'll see a big, bold sentence, reading: *Spoiler alert—you live.*

"No, the nine hundreds are *this* way." A sharp voice jolts me.

Peering over the yellowed pages of my book, I see Leslie Choi-Blankenship and Wei Li, who are looking through the stacks. I shouldn't be surprised—they're probably meeting up to research their project just like Cat and me. Also, I see Leslie at this library all the time. But it still feels as if she's invading my fortress of solitude. It also means I don't have any book-related psychic powers—or else I would have seen her coming.

The second Leslie spots me, she makes a face like she's smelling the world's most toxic fart. Then she and Wei start whispering. To Wei's credit, they glance at me with a flash of worry in contrast with Leslie's poorly concealed loathing.

Ah, well. Leslie probably came with Cat. While I wait for her, I can amuse myself.

"Look at that liar boy," I mutter under my breath, imitating Leslie. "I read this book on cancer once, and it's, like, a *really* serious disease. Someone should fire that boy out of a cannon into the sun."

"Oh, I don't know," I reply as Wei. "Is that too extreme?"

"Nope. Right into the sun," I go on, mimicking Leslie's prim, high voice. "My boyfriend, Kevin, can light the fuse and then hopefully that boy will explode into—"

"*Excuse* me?"

Uh-oh.

Cat Pellegrini stands over me, giving me this look like she's about to refer me to a hotline of some kind.

Shifting uncomfortably in my seat, I say, "Uh, hi." Maybe she didn't hear me. Maybe—

"Did you just say you hope that Leslie and Wei *explode?*" Cat demands.

"No, y-you don't understand. I was saying that *I* should explode," I scramble to explain. "Well, not really but uhhh . . ."

Cat knits her brow. "You were looking right at them, though," she says, sitting down across from me. Man, she is *not* letting this go. Her eyes widen as she says, "You're not one of those loner boys, are you? I hear scary things about loner boys. Like they're plotting something. I mean, no offense, but you're alone and you *are* a boy."

"Those things are both true," I say. Cat looks even more concerned. That may have sounded more ominous than I intended. Whoops. "Well, um, the *'alone'* and the *'boy'* part, not the 'plotting something' part." I squeeze my eyes shut and silently pray that this is the moment I get abducted by aliens.

She gives me a long, quizzical look. Oh no. Is she going to ask me about the note? I mean, clearly, I should bring it up. But I don't even know what I would say if she straight-up accused me of something.

Fortunately, Cat merely shakes her head and drops a pile of books on the table. "O-kay."

"Okay," I mirror her.

"Anyway, I found some books," she says, flipping her hair. *Again.* Why do girls always do that? Is it in their DNA? And, if hair is in their way so much, why don't they cut it?

I glance down, expecting to see a few basic books on earthquakes, but the pile is mostly thick, ancient-looking tomes.

"Did you find all these books here?" I ask.

"Yeah, why?"

I blow a cloud of dust off one of them. "On the *shelf*?"

Her eyes blink rapidly. "Umm, no. They're stored in the basement. I . . . called ahead."

She called ahead? Seriously? Whatever, I don't even care.

"All right," I say.

"Why don't you scan through these and see if you can find anything that would help us." She hands me a new-looking book that reads *Disasters to the Extreme!*

Shaking my head, I grab one of the dusty ones. "I'm actually into old books. There's probably more *primary sources*." I shoot her a meaningful look, because earlier it seemed like Cat wanted to marry primary sources.

Cat smiles ever so slightly, but then it reverts to a frown. She moves to take the whole stack, but I reach for one that's sandwiched between two thick books on top. It looks different from the others—more like a journal than a library book. When I take a closer look at the cover, I see a few stray doodles and Cat's name written in elaborate cursive.

"Is this another earthquake notebook?" I ask, turning it over in my hands. "Sweet baby Yoda, how many pages do you *have* on this?"

Cat's eyes go wide. Clearly, she didn't want me to see the book at all. "Give that back!"

"Why?" I counter. "If it's notes about the earthquake, I should read them too, right?"

"Give me . . . give me it!" She keeps swiping at me, but I hold the book over my head. Why am I being such a jerk? Even if someone was passing Cat that note, it's not as if *she* started the rumor. I should just ask her if it was Kevin and get it over with.

Guiltily, I hand the book back to her. "I'm sorry. But, hey, I need to ask you something about tomo—" I stop short when something falls out from between the pages of the book, fluttering to the floor. Cat takes the opportunity to grab it, but doesn't seem to have noticed the paper. Stooping, I pick it up.

Huh.

It's a printout of an article from a science magazine I've never heard of: *Science on the Fringe*. I unfold it and start to read the headline out loud: "'The irrefutable link between earthquakes and unidentified aerial phenomena—'" I raise my eyes to meet hers. "What—"

"*Not* yours!" Cat yells. She snatches the paper out of my hands, looking murderous.

I know now is the time for me to ask Cat about the note, but my mind is swirling with questions. Did that really say "unidentified aerial phenomena," as in UFOs?! Why would Cat be looking into *anything* like that? And why won't she let me see the article?

"I'm just looking up anything having to do with earthquakes," she explains in a pointed tone. "This is a big project and I don't want to leave any stone unturned. Even if it's totally ridiculous. You know?"

"Yeah. Ridiculous," I say carefully. "But . . . *kind of* interesting, don't you think?"

Cat's face flickers with an odd look, but then she lets out a disbelieving scoff. "It's interesting how many people need to make things up," she retorts coolly.

"Yeah, totally," I say, shifting uncomfortably on my chair. "Um, but why do you think they would make it up?"

Cat rolls her eyes. "Their lives are boring?"

I try not to flinch. "Sure. Only . . . how do you explain those lights people saw during earthquakes? That's what the article said, right?"

"EQLs?" Cat scoffs again. "I don't know. Can we get back on topic? We only have three weeks for this, and we want to get all of our material together before we write. It has to be *tight*."

"Sounds good," I say, but my mind is still running a mile a minute. If she thinks it's so ridiculous, why is she dropping the initialism for earthquake lights like she's an expert?

"Everything okay?" Cat asks.

"Mm-hmm," I mumble. But something feels off. For the first time since he died, it's like I almost feel Oscar over my shoulder, yelling at me to pay attention.

"Great. Let's make an outline." She pulls out the notebook I'd picked up earlier, flipping to a page in the back, but then grunts in frustration when the last page is filled. I don't care what she says, that writing is tiny. Serial-killer-vibes tiny.

I'm about to offer her one of my notebooks, when

she closes it and grabs a fresh blank one out of her back-pack. Okay, I guess she's just a research nerd.

As she tosses the other notebook to the side, my mouth goes suddenly dry. Now that I'm getting a closer look at the back side, I see another assortment of doodles and cartoons. Most of them fade into each other—a cat with cute chibi eyes, and a few geometric patterns. Until I see one sketch toward the bottom corner.

What the *what?*

Sure, it's not *identical.* The lines are neater, and it's more of a circle than an oval. And there's only one jag-ged line underneath. But it's close, right? Suddenly my skin is buzzing with I don't *know* what.

Is Cat Pellegrini sketching the same symbol from Oscar's last message?

CHAPTER
* 5 *

On the walk home, I'm so distracted, I barely notice ten minutes passing me by. Before I know it, I'm halfway down my street.

I can't stop thinking about that symbol, and all the stuff I want to look up when I get home. I'll start with a new web image search. Maybe if I redraw Cat's doodle from memory . . .

"Oh! Sam!" A surprised voice breaks my focus as I walk down the sidewalk toward my house. It's my neighbor, Mrs. Crutchley, with her husband not too far behind.

Weirdly, I don't think I've interacted with them in months—despite the fact that they live next door. Since Mom and Auddy have been driving me everywhere, I'm always going straight from the garage door to the car.

Turns out, having cancer makes you an indoor boy.

"Hey, Mr. and Mrs. Crutchley," I say, feeling oddly formal. "I was just walking home from the library."

"Walking? I would have thought—" Mr. Crutchley cuts himself off.

"Never mind that," Mrs. Crutchley says, a nervous edge creeping into her voice. "How . . . are you?" She tilts her head and nods sympathetically as if I've already told her a piece of bad news.

This is weird. I know from Mom and Auddy that the Crutchleys helped us set up a meal-delivery thing back in February when I started chemo. But that was months ago. Did they tell them about Oscar, too?

"I'm . . . fine," I tell them self-consciously. "Why?"

"I'm sure you know your mothers told us all about the . . ." Mr. Crutchley leans forward and whispers the word "cancer." The word comes out soft and heavy all at once, as if he's afraid the word itself will hear him.

"Yeah . . . um, I'm doing much better now," I mutter awkwardly. "Thanks, though."

"We're praying for you!" Mrs. Crutchley blurts out. "Every Sunday."

"Thank you?" It comes out like a question because I can't quite make heads or tails of this conversation. "I mean, thank you."

They exchange a relieved look. "Well, anyhow, we'll let you rest, honey."

How do I respond to that? I've got Mom and Auddy telling me I'm some kind of hero warrior, people at school thinking I'm a psychopath who lies about cancer, and now the Crutchleys are acting like I'm an invalid. Is this my life now?

"All right. Bye." I turn and walk up the path, my feet heavier all of a sudden. On one hand, *whatever*. The Crutchleys don't know me. Still, I need to take a beat before I go inside and tell Mom and Auddy about the note. I open the door as quietly as I can, so I can slip up the stairs and hide in the bathroom for a few minutes before they catch me.

As soon as I'm inside, however, I can hear their voices floating in from the family room.

". . . was only a ten- to twenty-percent chance, and that was early."

My heart races, and I freeze at the entryway. Are they talking about Oscar?

"We're so lucky. Poor Gabriel and Lilli. I can't even imagine what they're feeling. Glioblastoma can . . ." Mom erupts into a long string of words that I would get in trouble for using. She uses them a lot when cancer is the topic.

"I'm worried about Sam," Auddy's voice sounds in reply. "He says he doesn't want to go back to Chemo Kidz."

Ah, yes. Chemo Kidz. The weirdo therapy group where they make us shout our feelings and then dance to Disney songs under a strobe light. *Shudder*. It's a hard pass from me, but at least it's where I met Oscar.

"I never hear about any other friends at Northborough," Auddy goes on. "Since he met Oscar, he hasn't wanted to talk to anyone else. He doesn't talk to Kevin anymore, does he?"

I close my eyes.

That was my first lie of omission with Mom and Auddy. I never told them about *Kevin*.

An obsession with Mario Kart brought us together last year. Before long, he was spending weekdays at my house while I taught him how to get ahead in Fortnite as a professional bush camper. I thought that's what a friend *was*—having things in common. I mean, I was this weirdo loner kid, and Kevin always had other friends. But we ate lunch together at school. That's a friend thing, or so I thought. When I told him about my diagnosis, I don't know what I expected. It wasn't for him to just . . . leave. But that's exactly what he did.

I wasn't shocked when I saw it happen with my

online gamer friends. Over time, they messaged less and stopped tagging me to be on their team for Rocket League because they "figured I needed to rest." I mean, how do you deal with that when you don't know someone in real life? But Kevin was my *friend*. Wasn't he?

I shake the thought off, listening as Mom speaks up again. "I'm worried, Audrey. Today when I drove him to school, he seemed so . . . lost."

I slip off my shoes and skitter up the stairs to my room, not wanting to hear any more.

Maybe the reason you have no friends is because you're a weirdo freak.

Mom and Auddy are tired of having to deal with you.

Dr. Wrongbrain's cruel words cut into me, bubbling up from a deep, terrible place. Dude wants to torture me nonstop, and I'm *sick* of it.

"Stop it," I mumble, tears spilling out of my eyes.

Wrongbrain doesn't listen. The images come fast, and they quickly turn frightening. Oscar, lying in his ICU room. The way his skin looked like wax, as if he were a motionless action figure. His chest, moving jerkily up and down as the air pushed in . . .

Oscar went into the hospital in early August and was unconscious for two full weeks before we got the news. That night, I wasn't there. But every night before, Mom and Auddy let me go to the hospital and talk to him for as long as I had words. When I wasn't there, I brought in an old phone and told the Padillas to play my voice for him. Those two weeks felt like years. Plenty of time and material for Dr. Wrongbrain to use against me.

My whole body starts trembling, but a voice breaks through.

"Sam!" I hear Auddy call out. "Is that you? Are you home?"

My head jerks up, and I'm surprised to find that the sleeves of my hoodie are damp.

"Be right down!" I yell, hoping my voice sounds way more chill than I feel.

"Okay!" Mom yells. "We're starting dinner, so hustle!"

I allow myself three minutes to cry in my room. Any longer, and they'll see me.

"Oscar," I murmur. "I could really use you right about now."

To assassinate the nefarious Dr. Wrongbrain? Oscar says. *I'm in.*

I let out a surprise laugh. That might be the closest I've been to actually hearing him. It even sounded like his voice. I *am* getting better at this.

You know what I remember? How much you love that

episode of Otherworld with the phantom cat. It always calmed you down.

Make-believe Oscar is right. Fumbling for the remote, I scroll to an episode of *Otherworld* called "Deh-weles Arta." I let my eyelids close and speak the lines aloud.

"My dear Gemma. You've never heard of the Beast of Bodmin Moor?" I recite. "One of these days, you'll have to visit *my* section of the library."

It works.

"Thanks, Oscar," I whisper as I walk through my door.

When I round the corner to the top landing of the stairs, I see Auddy waiting at the bottom step. Her hair is still pulled back tightly in a twist, but she's down to a plain T-shirt and slacks—casual Friday for her.

"Hey!" she says. "Why didn't you come get us?"

"Just needed to hit the bathroom," I lie. The last lie, I tell myself.

"Well, come on. It's game night and Mom's making fried spaghetti—hurry up!"

Swallowing, I think about all the ways my news could ruin fried spaghetti night. If I tell them, what next?

"Somebody made up a rumor that I lied about having cancer." *Move back six spaces.*

Because that's what it would be. Moving back. *Again*.

There would be more long talks between Mom and Auddy while I sit alone in my room. Conversations about getting me back into therapy. Which means more appointments. And on and on. There would be less time for laughing, games, and TV marathons. And getting back to normal like we're *supposed* to be doing. See, this is the worst part about Big Things™. They're not your fault, but they ruin things as if they were.

So, I smile down at Auddy and break my own promise.

"Yeah, Auddy," I say. "School was great. I'll tell you everything."

CHAPTER
* 6 *

Every morning, I have a ritual.

    I wake up and wait for Mom and Auddy to start talking before I get out of bed. It began when I was going through treatment. Before cancer, I would wake up early and shuffle into their room right away. But, when treatment completely wiped me out, I slept later.

With my new wake-up time, I noticed something. I could hear Mom and Auddy's morning routine. Without me interrupting, they would talk and laugh.

It became like morning theater for me.

Sometimes, their routine happened over coffee downstairs. Other days, they would stay in bed and lounge (like "slug-o-beds," as Auddy would say). Today, I can hear their voices clear and booming from the kitchen downstairs. It's a coffee day. Sitting at the top of the stairs, I lean against the railing and smile as I listen.

"No, I would *never!*" Auddy is shouting. "You're thinking of yourself, my love."

Mom is teasing Auddy for saying a bad word. To be fair, this is an occasion for teasing, since Auddy is the polite and buttoned-up type. I snicker as I hear Mom chant the bad word over and over. She's probably poking Auddy too, which she hates.

I'm not going to make a whole deal out of it or anything, but it's awesome how they're, like, *really* in love. Not just in love, but *happy* with each other. Early on, I was really scared that I would die—not only because of the death part, but because of Mom and Auddy. What if I died and it ruined their whole life together? The thought of it has the same effect as the "Am I okay?" question—it ends up as this weight on me that grows until I'm tired.

Hearing them in the mornings makes that weight lift, if only a little bit.

"Saaaa-aaaammmm! We can hear you!" Mom calls. "You're being a creeper again."

"Okay, okay!" I laugh. "I'll be right down." I shamble like a sleepy zombie back into my room to put on a sweatshirt. Even though the weather is still late-summer hot, it's always cold in the morning on this side of the bay. But warming up hits me with another instinct: the overwhelming urge to crawl back into bed. Before I know it, my head is hitting the pillow.

Pure slug-o-bed. That's the life for me.

I lie there for a minute, staring at the posters on my walls. There's one of Nina Simone, obviously. There's one with a gaming unicorn, and a small stylized print from *Moana* that Auddy got me for my birthday. Then, of course, there's *Otherworld*.

Seeing the distressed and stylized UFO on the poster immediately brings my mind back to Cat and the symbol.

Hit with a burst of energy from the reminder, I sit up and grab my laptop. With everything that went down last night, I'd barely done any research. A basic image search of the symbol came up empty, so I type "EQL UFO earthquake symbol" into Google. Of course, way too *many* results pop up this time. After looking through a page or two of images, I let out a frustrated groan. It's mostly banner images from a few UFO websites and random conspiracy memes that Mom and Auddy would have a *lot* to say about.

You could just ASK that girl Cat about the symbol. My head pops up in surprise as I hear Oscar's voice again—this time without prompting.

"Um, no, I can't," I mutter aloud. It feels weird, talking to him like this when I don't have the excuse of a freak-out to explain it. But . . . it doesn't suck. "You know how I am around girls."

Just imagine you're James Baskerville talking to—

"Sam!" Auddy's voice breaks in. "Are you coming or what?"

"To be continued," I say under my breath. I glance around the room, just to make sure that my newfound make-believe Oscar isn't actually *there*—outside my head. Of course, there's nobody there. Frowning, I head downstairs.

Mom ruffles my curls when I sit at the table. "Morning, Baby Cricket."

"No, love! *Sam*," Auddy chides her. "I swear, that boy's going to move out the minute he's grown if you don't stop with that."

It's funny how different she and Auddy are. Mom is messy, with puffy light brown hair that always looks like it exploded. Although, to be fair, Mom is a pre-K speech therapist. It's hard to be neat when you sit on the ground with toddlers all day. Still, she would live in sweats if Auddy let her. Auddy is a lawyer, but her wardrobe is 24-7 professional. She even dresses in button-up shirts to go to the grocery store.

There are times I look at Auddy's corkscrew curls and imagine that I get my hair from her. Or my eyes—dark brown like Auddy's. I know she and Mom got together after I came along. Also, she's Black and I'm white (as in, pale as the tree of Gondor itself). Still, I hope Auddy thinks of me as hers. Some days I feel more hers than Mom's.

"So," Mom goes on. "Auddy and I were just saying how, despite the million questions we asked you about school, you managed to avoid answering even one with details."

"Uh-huh," I say, stalling as I grab a piece of fakin' bacon off the serving plate.

"'Uh-huh. School fine. Sam fine. Bacon good.'" Mom mimics me in a low voice that makes me sound like Frankenstein's monster.

Auddy leans forward, her hands clasped. "Seriously, aren't there any *highlights*?"

I gulp. "Um, yeah, actually. I mean, I wouldn't call it a highlight."

Immediately, Auddy blinks, and that crease forms between Mom's brows. I hate that crease. "Did something happen?" Auddy asks.

Okay, there it is, Sam. A direct question. And you have a direct answer. *I think someone is spreading a rumor that I'm lying about having cancer. I think that someone might be Kevin.*

Move back six spaces.

"They assigned us the California History Project," I hear myself saying instead.

"Oh! I heard about that," Mom says. She and Auddy trade a relieved look that sends an ache right through my gut.

"Who's your partner?" Auddy asks, eyeing me. "They pair you up, right?"

Pure Auddy. She doesn't badger me like Mom, but just stealth *knows* everything.

"Some girl named Cat," I say. "We got the Loma Prieta earthquake." There you go, Sam. Change the subject to the natural disaster. That will end this portion of the conversation.

"Is Cat nice?" Auddy asks.

No luck.

I give them the world's most noncommittal shrug. "Eh."

Mom rolls her eyes. "Okay. I can tell we're being Those Moms. Shut it down, Audrey."

Auddy gives me a secret smile. "Shutting it down."

I imagine Oscar smirking at me. *You can't make ME shut it down.*

I almost choke on my fakin' bacon. Is Oscar talking to me around my moms now? I rush to steer the subject away from Cat again. "We need to interview someone who was there. For the earthquake, I mean."

"You should interview Mom," Auddy tells me. "You have a good story, right, Arielle?"

"Oh, I have a story." Mom sweeps a dramatic hand to the side, as if showing off a headline. "I was nine years old. It was after soccer practice on Tuesday, October seventeenth. If I had been coming from Hebrew class only a day earlier, it's possible I would have been on the Cypress Freeway when it collapsed."

"Oh man," I say, frowning. "Were you in the car?"

Mom shoves an errant curl back into her hair tie. "Yep. We were rolling. Grandma Beth was driving us across a freeway overpass and I swear I could see a huge gap in the concrete when we finally passed. They closed the overpass an hour later, so it could have been true."

I suddenly wish I was taking notes. "Cool. Do you mind if I interview you later?"

"Of course! Do you want to videotape me?" Mom asks. "I'll even wear a suit, Sam."

"Oh-ho, you know what that means," Auddy says, cackling. "A suit, Sam. A *suit*. This is the offer of a lifetime. I have not seen this woman outside a sweat suit since the wedding."

I laugh. "Well, I wasn't going to ask you to wear a suit, but now I am."

All three of us bust up laughing at the thought of Mom in a suit, so hard that I feel a side stitch coming on. I move to grab my side, but then let my hand relax—ignoring the pain as we keep laughing.

"You okay, Sammy?" Auddy asks, noting my grimace.

The world's worst game board appears before me again. *I say it's a pain and Mom's worry crease comes back. Auddy stops laughing. And the moment is over. Just like if I tell them about Kevin and the note . . .*

I stare at my food. I know I should tell them. And I can tell them. But . . . I don't want to. I want that force field. Just for a little while longer.

"I'm all good," I say aloud. "Just spit out a piece of my breakfast. No biggie."

After we're done laughing at the idea of Mom in a suit and I inhale the last of my food, I get up and ask to be excused so I can get dressed. It won't take more than two minutes to throw on jeans and calm down my giant curls with water, but they don't need to know that.

Opening up my laptop, I go back to the search bar,

typing "unidentified aerial phenomenon + earthquakes + symbol." Then I limit the search to exclude social media sites. Still *way* too many results to focus my search.

"Ugh!" I grumble.

Right away, I hear Oscar clucking in a comical display of disapproval. *If you would just ask Cat about the symbol* . . .

"Maybe I don't *want* to," I say aloud. "What are the actual chances she knows anything? You heard what she said. She thinks people who see UFOs are making stuff up."

Or maybe you're too scared of Kevin to ask her anything.

I snort. "Kevin can dry up and blow away for all I care."

If you say so.

"Oh, come on, Oscar!" I laugh. Then, hearing distant footsteps, I lower my voice. "Why are you busting me? All I'm doing is looking. *'Keep looking.'* That's what you said."

When I don't hear a reply, I sigh and stand to grab my backpack. "Sorry, dude. You know I love you, but there are limits to what I'll do. There's no way I'm going to talk to Cat-hecking-*Pellegrini* about aliens again."

CHAPTER
* 7 *

If my life were a movie, this is the point where the narrator would say: *Sam spent the next two days trying to talk to Cat-hecking-Pellegrini about aliens again.*

Wednesday went by and, since we didn't have a scheduled meeting, I kept *almost* approaching Cat. In the morning, she breezed past me before I had time to open my mouth. At lunch, I walked by her table and came *this* close to saying something. But then I saw Kevin heading toward us. Cat, Zooey, and Leslie had all turned to look at me, but I backed away awkwardly—like that GIF Mom always sends me of Homer Simpson disappearing into a bush.

On the plus side, most people weren't staring at me anymore. The whole school was buzzing about some kid who was sent home for writing something in the boys' bathroom. Nobody knew what he wrote—and everyone knows it would have to be bad to keep you out of school—so it was all anyone could talk about.

Well, except for Leslie.

I still caught her whispering every time she looked at me. And, every time I so much as glanced in *her* direction, she shot me a look I can only describe as a death glare.

By this morning, I'd convinced myself that Cat isn't remotely worth it. It's like I told Oscar: What could someone who clearly doesn't believe in UFOs know about them? And that symbol could be nothing more than a random assortment of shapes—a total coincidence.

Still, as I sit in social studies at the end of the day, I find myself mindlessly doodling in my sketchbook and wondering how to approach her next.

You are the KING of side quests, I hear Oscar say in my ear. *You can do this. Just open your mouth and talk to the girl.*

I smile. So he isn't giving up on me yet.

I'm sorry, is talking to some random girl a side quest? I ask him silently.

Sam Kepler Greyson. Talking to a human girl is the ONLY noble side quest.

Dude. You're one to talk, I think. *You never said a word to that girl Jaymee from Chemo Kidz with the purple scarf and pink fuzz cut.*

Oscar strokes his pale and hairless chin wisely in my mind. *This is true. But—*

"Hey, Sam." Cat Pellegrini rips me out of my alternate reality with two words.

I look up at her, slack-jawed.

Then, my backpack strap slips through my fingers and the whole thing falls. I watch as every last item spills out across the floor. It's one of those truly nightmare scenarios, where each crashing item is louder than the last. Then, just when you think it's over, one last thing drops with a loud *clang.*

I swear I can actually hear Oscar laughing his butt off.

". . . Sam?" Cat repeats it like it's a question.

Clang.

This time, I do hear Kevin laugh. But, when I look up, he's already turned away.

"Ummm." I close my eyes and try to reset. Reset and act like the last two minutes never happened. "Yeah. Hey, Cat. Same time after school?"

Okay, that was better. Oscar would even say so.

Short sentences. No extraneous information. *Super* laid-back. Exactly like Baskerville.

"So, that's the thing," Cat says, grabbing a chunk of hair and wrapping it tightly around her index finger. "I forgot to tell you, and then you disappeared yesterday."

"Sorry about that," I say. "I . . . had to get home."

She gives me a searching look. "Anyway. I have to stay late for cheer practice today."

I try not to sound disappointed. "So . . . you need to cancel?"

"No," she says. "But can you meet me at four thirty? That way I can run home fast and change before I go to the library. We'll still have until six."

"No problem," I say, even though it kind of *is* a problem. What am I supposed to do for an hour and a half?

She nods. "Great. I'll see you at the library."

I take in a long breath and exhale. "See you there."

After school, I decide to walk to the library early to get a good table. It's not as if I have anything better to do. However, as I walk up the path, I see that the entryway is dark.

"Huh," I say aloud. "That's weird." Usually, the library

is open every day except for Sunday. Peering at the double doors, I see a large sign on the window:

CLOSED FOR INVENTORY

Great.

What am I supposed to do? Wait here for an hour, only to tell Cat we can't study here? I would call her, but she hasn't given me her phone number yet.

Suddenly, I remember something. Cat lives in our neighborhood. I know because, last December, the Pellegrinis sent Mom and Auddy a warning that we weren't meeting the homeowner's association "holiday decorating standard."

Apparently, the neighborhood goes all out for Christmas. Outdoor trees, lit-up candy canes, hanging snowflakes. It's as if Santa himself annually barfed over the whole fifteen-block radius. No inflatable menorahs or dreidels to be found, but maybe I can't complain when the only Hanukkah tradition my family honors is of the triple-fried-latke variety.

Anyhow, I remember Auddy brandishing the notice.

"I'm sorry, is this woman *requiring* that we put up Christmas decorations?"

"I like Christmas lights," my mom had said, pouting. As usual, she was completely unconcerned about our Jewish heritage. "They're so blinky and colorful!"

Laughing at the memory, I wonder what the *opposite* of devout is. Because Mom is that.

The warning notice, equal parts cheery and threatening, had the Pellegrinis' address on it. I don't remember the house number, but I know what block. Fifteen-hundred-something Cedar.

Without really deciding one way or another, I find myself wandering over to Cedar Avenue. Cat *did* say she would ask her parents about us studying there, so it's not like my showing up will be a total shock. It couldn't hurt to walk down the street, right? As it turns out, I don't need the exact address. After walking past only five houses on Cedar, I see an ornately trimmed mailbox that reads: *The Pellegrinis.*

Taking a deep breath, I walk up and knock on the door. Of course, as soon as I do, I realize I've made a huge mistake. What good can come of this? I should turn around and—

"Hello?"

—leave before anyone sees that I'm here.

Oh well.

A lanky girl with dark hair and light olive skin smiles from the doorway. She looks a little like Cat, but older and with more makeup. "Can I help you?"

"Ummm-I-um—" I stutter. Well done, Sam. That's some top-notch talking there.

She's starting to look bored. "Yes?"

"Does Cat live here?" I blurt.

She immediately regards me with suspicion, which I get. I *am* skulking in their front yard as if I'm casing the place for a robbery. "And you are . . . ?" she prompts me.

"Sam Kepler Greyson," I say, as if she needs to know my entire birth name. "I'm Cat's partner for the California History Project?"

Good job making your inflection go up at the end, Sam. Make it sound like a question. Brilliant.

"Oh!" Her golden-brown eyes widen. "I heard about that. Anyway, Cat's at cheer, but she's usually back by four. You can wait for her if you want. I'm Gia, by the way, Cat's sister."

I step into the house awkwardly, looking around. "Nice to meet you," I say.

"You can sit on the couch," Gia says. "I've just got to get back to a phone call, okay?"

After I nod my head yes, Gia smiles, flips her hair, and bounces to the next room. More hair flipping. Guess it's genetic. When I can't see her anymore, I sit down on the sectional sofa.

Wow. Everything is so . . . *white* here. With my dark hoodie and filthy shoes, I feel like a cloud of dirt in human form, threatening every pristine surface. Then, the second Gia disappears, I realize I have to pee.

I check my watch. Three forty-five. I still have time before Cat comes home. Tentatively, I creep toward the kitchen, where I see a clean white stove. Sweet merciful Wario, that's a lot of white. I find Gia talking into her phone at the kitchen table.

"Um, bathroom?" I ask, trying not to do a pee-jig.

Gia puts a hand over her phone and smiles at me. "The kittens are in the downstairs one, and it's a nightmare. We're fostering—long story. Why don't you head upstairs? It's straight ahead when you get to the top."

"Thanks!" I manage, before breaking into a jog upstairs and into the bathroom.

When I'm done, I can't help but look around. Makeup bags and scattered feminine products litter the countertop and a bra hangs from the hook on the door. Even though I have two moms and therefore see bras every day, my face flushes at the sight.

After I wash my hands, I head back to the stairs, stopping short when something catches my attention. The door at the end of the hall is painted a deep violet—a noteworthy change from the rest of the monochromatic house. I do a double take when I see what's hanging on the door: a distressed replica of the Area 51 sign. It doesn't actually *say* "Area 51," but I recognize the ominous wording that says "US Air Force Installation; Photography Is Prohibited."

"What the what?" I ask aloud, feeling drawn to the door as if it has its own tractor beam. There's no way this is Cat's room, so it must be Gia's.

Although . . . Cat *does* have a bazillion pages of earthquake notes and an article about UFOs. And there's that symbol. I know she said it was "ridiculous" and that people who have UFO stories are only making up for their "boring lives," but could she have been lying?

Gulping, I test the doorknob. It opens easily—too easily—and lets out a loud creak that threatens to totally narc on me.

Oh no. No, no, no. I can't do this. *Run away, Sam!*

Desperately, I change course and push the door closed, only to have the door bounce off the latch and rebound on me. Now, my sliver of visibility has become a wide-open door. I flinch, half expecting something terrible to be waiting for me but, when I tentatively peer in, I can't help but step inside.

No interplanetary monsters lie beyond the door, but it *does* look like a portal to another reality. The room is *exploding* with nerdiness. A cute stuffed alien sits on Cat's bed. Her closet door is open and inside I see a line of plain clothes, followed by a bunch of colorful costumes. Her lamp is a *Millennium Falcon* replica and . . . wait. Is that a *Star Trek* communicator badge? But that's not even the most mind-blowing part.

Past a series of recent pictures of Cat with Leslie and Zooey, I see a poster. It hangs right at the head of the bed—prime real estate for any room, and it features two familiar faces. On the glossy surface is a classic shot: James Baskerville aiming a flashlight into oblivion, while Gemma Monroe poses with a phase disturber.

Cat Pellegrini likes *Otherworld*.

Cat PELLEGRINI likes OTHERWORLD.

CAT PELLEGRINI—

"What are you doing in my room?!" a shriek sounds behind me.

Oh no . . .

Petrified, I turn around. Cat stands in the doorway, crossing her arms over her Northborough Niners cheer sweatshirt and looking like she's thinking of at least twelve ways to murder me.

CHAPTER
* 8 *

One of the things we talked about in my old therapy group, Chemo Kidz, was our instincts. I already knew the major ones: fight and flight. But our therapist taught us another one: *freeze*.

Ralphie, the therapist, was unbearably cringe. Example: he would wear these shirts that said things like "I *Can*-cer Vive," or "Believe in Your #Selfie." His never-ending positivity made me want to be a total bummer, if only to prove him wrong. He talked to us in a loud, bright voice as if cancer reverse-aged us back to preschool. It goes without saying that Oscar and I *hated* Ralphie. That said, his words about instincts ring in my head as Cat's blazing eyes land on me.

Because I *cannot* move.

"*Well*?!" she practically shrieks. "What are you doing here?"

"*OTHERWORLD*!" I yell, much louder than I mean to.

"What did you say?" she spits out angrily.

"Ummm, I was just walking down the hall and I saw the *Otherworld* poster."

"No, you didn't," she says, calling me out on my obvious lie. "I never leave my door open."

"I did! I saw it!"

It's ridiculous, but I feel committed to this lie now. The lie and I will eventually marry, have lying children, and settle down in a house very much like this.

"What's with all the noise?" another voice sounds. I see Gia peer in through the door.

Cat's pale olive skin is turning cotton-candy pink. "*He* said that my door was open."

"You never leave your door open," Gia says.

Oh god, oh god, oh god. Why, *why* can't I be "flight"? Why can't I sprout wings, like the pterodactyl people that Baskerville and Monroe discovered living in the caves of Scotland?

Both Gia and Cat stare me down.

"I'm really s-sorry," I sputter, looking around

desperately. "I did open your door. I swear, I'm not creepy. I saw that Area 51 sign and . . . hold on. Let me back up. After I saw that thing in your journal—"

Cat presses a hand to her face. "You read my journal?"

Why will no one murder me?

"No! The article that fell out!" I insist. Then, seeing her expression, I hang my head in defeat. "You know what? You're right. There's no explanation. I totally invaded your privacy. I didn't mean to, but clearly I did. I'm really sorry, okay?"

Cat's face softens ever so slightly. "Why were you here at all?" she asks. "We were supposed to meet at the library."

"The library was closed, and I remembered your address from that holiday tree order form," I explained clumsily. "I figured I should wait here for when you came home after cheer."

"Upstairs?"

Gia winces, looking over at me. "He had to use the bathroom, Caty. And you know the downstairs bathroom is—"

"—full of kittens," Cat finishes, face-palming. She sits on her bed, and Gia steps back toward the door.

"Um, I'm gonna let y'all figure this out, 'kay?"

She closes the door and I find myself alone again with my leading cause of death: a very, *very* angry girl. And I dealt with cancer, so . . . do that math.

Cat frowns, her hazel eyes downcast. For the first time, I notice that she has a constellation of freckles across her nose. It reminds me of Cassiopeia.

No, Sam! Stop noticing things that don't matter. *Just. Say. Words.*

"Ummm," I say intelligently.

Then, Cat says the last thing I expect. "Are you going to tell Leslie and Zooey that you saw my room?"

Huh?

I stare at her in confusion. It sounds like she's asking if I'll reveal some terrible secret. "No? I mean . . . wait. Tell them what about your room?" I ask.

"That you saw it and I'm a big old nerd."

I mean, she is. Maybe nerdier than I am. But why is that a problem? My eye catches on a print with an anime-style character that reads *Yeah, Alchemy!* and she sees me looking.

"It's Vierro from *Moon Tower*," she tells me. "Great show, but it's only my second-favorite after . . ." She trails off, gesturing to the Baskerville and Monroe poster.

"After *Otherworld*?" I say, shaking my head with confusion. She looks a little offended, so I rush to add, "I'm sorry, I'm just surprised. I've never even seen you wear a logo other than the one on your cheer uniform."

Cat crosses her arms. "Um, way to stereotype, *Samuel*. Cheerleaders can be nerds."

"I know cheerleaders can be nerds," I say. "But *you* don't act like a nerd. Look at that girl Rose Pfupajena from core class. She's on the cheer team, but that doesn't stop her from putting Thor flair all over her backpack."

"You're weirdly observant. Did you break into *Rose's* room, too?" she says with a snort.

Throwing my hands up, I say, "No, I sit right next to her in class! She writes 'Rose Hemsworth-Pfupajena' on every one of her notebooks."

Cat and I trade looks for a beat, and then we both laugh.

"I'm really sorry I went into your room," I tell her again. "I mean it."

She sighs. "Thanks. I guess we're okay."

"And I won't tell Leslie or Zooey anything if you don't want me to," I add. "But . . . don't they *know* what your room looks like? Or do you hide everything behind a secret wall?"

"They've never been over," she says quietly.

This blows my mind. "Huh?"

Cat shrugs. "At first, I always had an excuse. I

eventually told them my parents are really strict. Which is . . . only half true. They stopped asking after a while."

"I still don't get it," I confess. "Being a nerd or fangirl isn't a bad thing. Why would you walk around pretending to be boring when you're really like this?"

"Hey!" she protests.

"What?"

"I don't know. Wasn't that meant to be offensive?"

I shrug. "I guess the boring part was."

Cat shakes her head, but she lets out a giggle. "Were you born without a social filter?"

"Yes, it's true," I deadpan. "I suffer from social filtritis." It's basically true. I mean, I haven't had this long of a conversation with someone my age since . . .

You replacing me already, bro? I imagine Oscar saying with a grin.

Every detail comes immediately into focus and it's like I'm back in his room—there's his blue-striped sheets and the expansive bookshelf lining the wall by his bed. I can practically smell Oscar's nacho-cheese breath as he adds, *She's cute. Not as cute as me, though.*

I let out a snort in reply. But then, when I look back down, my picture of Oscar turns fuzzy and Cat's face replaces it like I've flipped through to another reality.

She looks baffled. "Hey, are you in there?"

"Oh, nothing," I say. "Just zoned out. My imagination runs off without me sometimes."

Was this Oscar only in my imagination? Suddenly I'm not so sure. But . . . no. It's not like Oscar is snark-haunting me. I'm just getting better at it, I guess.

Cat lets out a nervous and humorless laugh. "You sure you're not laughing at me?"

My eyes pop. "What? No, sorry it sounded that way. Why would you think that?"

Cat grabs her stuffed alien, hugging him to her chest. "I guess . . . because I don't know you that well. Maybe this is some big joke to you. You know?"

I wrack my mind for the best response. "I can promise you that it's not?" I say with uncertainty.

Cat shrugs.

"Wait!" I say. "What if I tell you all *my* nerd stuff? Then you'll have leverage over me, too." *Not that I really care*, I think. But I keep that inside.

A smile breaks out over her face. "Like, we compare dork scars? All right."

"Okay, okay . . ." I mumble, searching my mind. I don't have to search far. "Yes! In fourth grade, after I started watching *Otherworld* with Mom and Auddy, I made my own spaceship out of tinfoil and wooden skewers."

Cat laughs. "I've got you beat. I made up my own *language*."

I quickly counter, "*I* went around after the tinfoil incident telling people I was an alien replicant."

"What? No, you didn't!"

"And that nobody should tell my parents I replaced the real Sam." I lean back, grinning smugly, and she lets out a slow clap.

"Well done," she says. "I'm impressed."

"So, will you tell me, then? Why the act? It can't only be about Leslie and Zooey."

A cloud passes over her face. "No. It's not."

I try to sound neutral as I ask, "Then what is it?"

Cat stares at her hands, looking sad. "Well, a few years ago, everything changed."

Oh man. Was I too pushy just then? I'm so bad at people sometimes. A second ago, we were laughing, but then I brought the whole room down like a big cancer cloud. Should I make a joke? Ask her if everything changed when the fire nation attacked? There has to be *something*.

All I manage to come up with is, "Changed how?"

Cat shrugs. "When I was little, it was cute. But I got older and, all of a sudden, people started treating me like I was this big freak. People at school. My parents, too. I think they expected me to be a 'regular girl' who thinks about 'regular girl' things. When I didn't, everyone acted like it was a problem that needed fixing—as if I had bad wiring."

I wince. "Yikes. What *do* regular girls think about?"

Cat throws her hands up in frustration. "I don't know. Nail polish?"

"Does anyone really *think* about nail polish?"

"Maybe if they love nail polish."

I point at her. "But you don't."

"How do you know?" she sputters. "Maybe I love it more than anything!"

My head might explode. "But . . . you said you didn't! Just now. You said everyone expected you to be a regular girl who likes nail polish, but you're not."

Cat looks thoughtful. "One time I got black polish with little Chewbacca heads. That wasn't so bad. But it's not *girly*-girly."

"Hey," I say, putting my hands up. "Nail polish doesn't have to be a gender thing. My moms paint my nails all the time when they're bored, and I'm extremely masculine, so . . ."

She leans forward, suddenly interested. "Really?! What color do they use?"

I smack my hand to my forehead, moaning. "Ahh!

Are we trapped in a horrible time loop? One in which only nail polish exists?"

We lose it, laughing for a few minutes until I decide to try again. "So, if you don't like things like *nail polish*, why do you pretend to?"

She shrugs. "When I left Saint Chris and transferred to Northborough, I thought: new school, new attitude. At school, I like what the other girls like. I talk about what they talk about. It's . . . easier."

"But isn't that tiring?"

She looks down, not saying anything.

"It sucks that you feel like you have to pretend," I say. "I would hate it if people expected me to be some kind of stereotypical *guy* guy." My mind suddenly flashes back to Kevin.

"Why are you wearing a Moana *shirt?"* my (ex-)friend had asked me one day.

"Because Moana *is awesome,"* I said with a shrug.

"Whatever, bro," Kevin had scoffed.

He didn't say anything else, but his opinion was obvious. Wearing a shirt with a Disney princess on it wasn't what *guys* did. It was different. *I* was different. And Kevin always acted like he was doing me this big favor by gaming with me—being friends with the school loser. After that, I didn't wear the shirt around him ever again.

I push the memory away.

"Hey, Cat?" I say carefully. Because it's now or never. I need to ask her about the symbol. Even though I know that we're both into the UFO thing, I can't help expecting her to pull off a mask and tell me I'm being pranked. But I have to try. Nervously, I grab the hooded alien plush on Cat's bed and fidget with it. "I kind of need to ask you something—"

"Hey!" she protests. "Hands off Jorge."

I look down at the plush and back up at her. "Jorge?"

"Aliens have names," she tells me, grinning sheepishly.

"That's fair." I take a deep breath. "So . . . here goes. Why are you trying to find a link between earthquakes and UFOs?"

Cat's jaw drops. For a full moment, she seems incapable of speech, but then she finally sputters, "H-h-how did you know that?"

I fidget with the sleeve of my hoodie in Jorge's absence. "Well, first, it was sort of obvious that you cheated to get the Loma Prieta quake. You already had a novel's worth of notes on it, and there's no way you had that much on *every* possible topic. So, I figure you helped Ms. Wong with the papers and folded them differently or whatever. At the library, you somehow had all of these books reserved from the history room. There was the article about earthquake lights—EQLs or whatever—and UFOs. Then . . . there's the symbol."

Cat looks taken aback. "What symbol?"

I reach over and grab a blank piece of lined paper and a pen from her desk to sketch it out. "You doodled it in your notebook. The one with your Loma Prieta notes."

Cat's eyes go wild. "Wait. You know Foo Fighters?"

"I . . . think my mom listens to them," I say, confused by her reply.

"What? No. 'Foo Fighters' is another phrase for 'UFOs.' It's a website." Cat grabs her laptop and, a moment later, shows me the screen. The symbol pops up, as clear as day, in the banner of an email addressed to Cat called "Personal Encounters."

"Whoa," I say, scanning the first few lines. "How did this not pop up in my web search?"

"Some sites take precautions to hide their content from basic web searches to protect their users," Cat tells me. "UFOs—it's still a stigma, you know? But, to answer your question, this isn't from a post. It's been in a couple of the emailed newsletters. I don't know *what* the symbol is, really—I just doodled it."

"Well, who writes the newsletters?" I ask. "Maybe they'll know what the symbol is."

Cat frowns at the screen. "It doesn't say. But I can ask. Hold on, I'll DM the moderators."

As she types something out on her phone, I peer at the screen, reading the top of the newsletter. "Oh wow, this story is from Tokyo," I say. "That huge earthquake in 2011."

"Yep," Cat says. "The guy said he saw the lights change shape as the ground shook, almost like a distortion."

"That kind of reminds me of the UFO Baskerville saw after he got Monroe out of the SIS facility," I say. "Of course, Gemma came too late. As usual."

Cat rolls her eyes. "Ugh, right? I hate that. Why is she so skeptical when it's *obvious* Baskerville is right?"

I clear my throat, but don't reply. I actually love that about Gemma, but now isn't the time. "So, you never answered me. Why are you studying a UFO-earthquake connection at all?"

Cat bites her lip, but then looks up tentatively to face me. "I can explain," she says. "But I need to show you something first."

CHAPTER
* 9 *

A half hour later, Cat and I are standing at an ornate stone archway that reads *Don Francisco Cemetery* and I can't say I'm happy with her choice of venue.

"Really? You need to show me a graveyard?" I ask dubiously.

"Yeah."

I furrow my brow. "You need to show me *this* specific graveyard. Not Oak Park, or Sacred Fart, or—"

Cat chokes out a laugh. "You mean Sacred Heart?"

"Anyone who calls it that is missing an opportunity," I retort, shivering. "Anyhow, it's cold and I don't like . . ." I stop myself before I can say "I don't like graveyards" because that would lead us right back to cancer, and that horrible note.

"Sam?" Cat asks. "You don't like . . . ?"

"Never mind," I say breezily, pushing Cat's question to the side. Bringing up the note now will derail whatever Cat wants to show me, and I'm still not even sure I want to ask her about it.

Cat motions to a cluster of benches overlooking the endless line of headstones. "Here, sit," she says ominously. Or maybe everything sounds ominous in a cemetery.

I stare up the slope, spotting the not-so-famous sign hill of our town that reads: *South San Francisco: The Industrial City.* Then I look back at Cat. "Okay, should I be worried? You asked me to come here and now you're not saying anything."

She laughs nervously. "Sorry, I should have explained on the way. I'm not used to talking about this stuff. Anyway, see that tunnel of trees?"

I follow her glance past a row of headstones lining the walkway in front of us and see what she means. The pathway just up the hill is lined with trees, their branches reaching toward each other like outstretched hands. "Yeah."

"A little over two years ago, there was this earthquake. It was only a 5.0 but—"

"I remember that!" I exclaim. It was in fifth grade, and I can still see the ceiling fan over our old dining table shuddering. "It wasn't that big, but I think it was right under us."

"I felt it too," Cat says. She pauses for a second before going on. "Anyway, right after that earthquake there was a UFO sighting. Right here at Don Francisco Cemetery."

"Really?" I ask. "How do you know about it?"

Cat's face twitches. "I saw a video on YouTube right after the earthquake. The person wasn't able to catch it on camera, but I could feel it—they were telling the truth."

"I'm on YouTube nonstop, but I never saw it. Can you show me?"

"Unfortunately, I can't. When I tried to show Gia a few hours later, someone had deleted it," Cat tells me. "Probably the original poster did it fast, or it would have been shared."

"So, how did you find it?" I ask. "If it didn't go viral or get shared out."

Cat shifts uncomfortably. "I was already into UFOs and I . . . tend to get pretty obsessed when I get on a topic. Anyway, the lights appeared over that tunnel of trees, and it sounded like so many other accounts. The guy said it was almost as if these big spotlights were flipping on, one after another. Then, darkness and a loud pulsing hum." Her hazel eyes flick toward me.

I'm suddenly rooted to the bench. "Go on," I encourage her.

"Really?"

"Um, yeah!" I show her my arm. "See? Goosebumps."

Cat's eyes light up, and I feel as if I passed a test. Her shoulders drop, relaxed, and she turns to me excitedly. "He said he followed the lights all the way through the trees. Then, he saw it—a big ball of light, with this halo of greenish blue around it. It was real low, and far back by the hill so you had to be in the right spot to see it. But then . . . it *disappeared*."

"Whoa!" I exclaim a bit too loud. Worried we could bother actual mourners, I lower my voice. "But it's kind of weird, right? Why would aliens come to sign hill? I mean . . ." I sweep my hand toward it. "It's like the Hollywood Sign but not interesting at *all*."

"I think it was the earthquake," Cat says, her voice rising excitedly. "If there *is* a connection between them, it makes sense."

I'm not so sure it makes sense. The earthquake was only 5.0 on the Richter scale, which is a thousand times less energy than a big quake like the Loma Prieta. Why would aliens prioritize a nothing earthquake in a nothing city? I don't say any of this, though. She seems reluctant enough to tell me this stuff. I shouldn't Gemma out on her yet.

"It's interesting for sure," I say neutrally. "But I still don't get why you went into stealth mode to get the Loma Prieta quake when you could get any of this information online. You don't need permission to research it."

She stares at the grass. "Yeah, I guess I didn't need to."

"Why, then? Was it to get access to those old books? It seems like a lot of trouble to—"

"My parents check my search history!" she blurts out, cutting me off.

"They do?" This blows my mind. Mom and Auddy have never checked my search history. Right? Yikes, I hope not.

Cat looks frustrated. "I shouldn't have said that. It's . . . complicated with my parents, but I'd rather not talk about that now. Okay?"

"Suuuuure," I say hesitantly. Part of me wants to ask more, but I can't exactly judge her for keeping it to herself when I'm going out of my way not to talk to her about quite a bit. "So, what have you found on the UFO-earthquake connection so far?"

Cat lets out a long sigh. "I've been reading a bunch of articles and blogs, but there's so many different viewpoints. Some people say EQLs are real, and that aliens might be studying how our planet works. But then, for every article I find saying they're real, there are three articles from scientists who say that EQLs are a natural oddity, like the aurora borealis."

"That's what I saw too," I say. "My best fr—" I cut myself off before I finish.

"Your best friend?" she prompts me with a curious look.

The consequences of finishing that sentence blink at me in blinding lights. "Um, my best friend and I used to study this stuff too. UFOs, aliens. He always said that the conflicting facts and stigma of it keep us from scientific progress."

Cat sighs. "I *wish* I had a friend like that." Her eyes cloud over. "Who is he? Does he go to Northborough?"

My heart beats faster. The truth is still this big, immovable thing between us, and I keep telling myself to just tell her already. But if I tell her about Oscar, what comes next?

"Sam?" Cat nudges me.

"He doesn't go to Northborough," I say before I can stop myself.

Cat blinks. "But if he knows about this stuff, maybe he could help. We could text him—"

"No," I cut her off quickly. "We can't text him. It's . . . um . . . complicated." Okay, it's not too late. Just tell her. It won't be that hard. And she's nice. Just open your mouth and *say it*.

"Oh, is he only an online friend?" Cat says, understanding washing over her face. "Hey, don't be embarrassed. I've got those too. What about his socials? Does he have Instagram?"

"I don't use anything like that," I tell her. "My moms say I'm better off avoid—"

I break off when she looks at me like *I'm* an alien.

"No Insta? Wow. Are your parents super strict about socials?"

"It's not like that," I explain. "They only told me what I might run into. A bunch of hate— homophobia and antisemitism and all that. I'd . . . rather not, you know?"

Cat gives me a long look that sets my nerves on end. "I get it," she says slowly. "And, speaking of . . . stuff like that, I wanted to mention something about that note. From Tuesday."

Oh no. I never thought she would bring it up. I suddenly feel like a trapped animal, desperately looking for a clear exit. "Y-yeah?"

She takes a deep breath. "I know you saw what it said, and I just want you to know . . . I don't think people really believe it. Well, *I* don't. Not now, at least."

I slump over, my muscles relaxing one at a time from the top down like I'm a melting ice cube. It sounds like she already knows I didn't lie. Which also means—

"Yeah. I mean, it got around last year that you were sick with something, but I don't know why Kevin said you lied about having *cancer.*"

"I don't know," I say robotically. So it *was* Kevin. But . . . wait. Does Cat actually know I didn't lie? She said "sick with *something.*" But she didn't say what.

"A ton of people were on independent study over the winter because of the Covid surge, either because they got it, or they had something else chronic." She blinks at me. "Was it something like that? Did you end up with Covid?" She's making it seem like that would be the normal answer, which makes sense. Tons of people got Covid last year, and nobody had a serious case that I knew of.

"Something . . . like that," I say carefully.

"It's a weird thing for him to make up out of nowhere," Cat says. "I hope you don't let it get to you. At least it sounds like you have friends outside of school, so . . ." She trails off.

Have friends. *Have.* She's making all the wrong assumptions, and I know I should clarify. But there's that game again.

"Actually, I do have cancer. And he's not an online friend. He died last month." Move forward two spaces and collect a new character—Sympathy Cat.

No more fun, no more comparing dork scars. I would tell her I have cancer. And that my friend isn't, in fact, online, but two cemeteries over. And then she would get that look.

I know Cat isn't Kevin. She's *nice*, for one. But what if telling the truth changes everything about the future? What if it makes her totally different? In the last few hours, I've even had moments of forgetting about this horrible year. It's almost like . . . being a normal kid.

"I don't have that friend anymore," I tell her haltingly in one breath. "Not because he's an online friend. He just, um, doesn't want to be my friend anymore."

The lie comes out way too easily. Actually, technically it's *two* lies. And they're big. Big lies for Big Things™. It's not only keeping information to myself, or saying I'm "fine" when I'm not. All of a sudden, I'm afraid I've sparked a flame and I'm watching it burn out of control.

Dr. Wrongbrain is the first to catch fire, sending me pictures of Oscar, flashing rapidly until I feel myself wince. He sends me a vision of Oscar in the hospital bed, saying, "Why would you say I wasn't your friend?"

The picture is different from the Oscar I've been seeing and hearing. He looks worse. Smaller. More frail.

"He ghosted you? That sucks, I'm sorry," Cat says. "I've been there." She seems to have accepted all of it with two vague statements. Could it really be that easy?

"It is what it is," I say.

It's literally the opposite of what I said. But I can't ignore the relief coming over me in waves. I feel safer now. What is *wrong* with me?

"Um, anyway," I go on, "before he left, we made this book together. It tracked sightings across the US. After he was gone, I saw this weird doodle I didn't recognize. When I saw that you drew one that looked so similar, I had to ask you." I reach behind me to shrug off my back-pack and grab the *Guide to Finding Intelligent Life*. Then I open it to the last page.

"'We are not alone in the universe,'" Cat reads aloud after I hold it up. My arms break out in goosebumps as she scrutinizes me. "It's weird. Why would he write this, and then ghost you?"

"I—I, um . . ." A tinkling notification sound breaks in, saving me from having to bungle another lie I can't come back from.

Cat glances at her phone. "Hey, look, I got a response

already from Foo Fighters!"

"About the symbol?" I ask, sidling up next to her.

"No, just a list of the people who write the newsletters. The mods take turns with it, so it could be any of them. Maybe we can message each of them to ask if they recognize it?" She hands me her phone and I read a list of nonsensical anonymous handles.

"Not exactly helpful," I murmur, scrolling until one username pops out at me. Huh. When I see one name, I can almost zero in on something. It's not quite a memory; more of . . . an echo.

"Sam? Do you see something?" Cat asks.

I click the profile that reads R0wanc@Fitzw1ll1am and look at the profile. Nothing specific jumps out, but my mind races. Grunting in frustration, I hand Cat back her phone.

Oscar whispers in my ear. *Remember how I used to write things in the margins?*

"Wait," I say out loud, holding up a finger to Cat. I grab the book again and flip to the front. "I want to check something. Oscar used to write in the margins of our old notes."

"That's his name? Your friend who ghosted you?"

I don't reply. The irony of her using the word "ghosted"

is not lost on me. But I can't think about that now. I skim through the margins until I get to the entries we made a few weeks before the end. "Look!" I say, pointing at Oscar's messy scrawl:

Tell Sam we need to talk to RC Fitzwilliam at CFK

"I don't know what 'CFK' means but, look. RC Fitzwilliam! And this user handle. If you change all the ones to letters, it's definitely Rowan C. Fitzwilliam. That has to be the same person, right?" I exclaim.

"Does that mean your . . . um, old friend was in contact with this moderator?"

"Not necessarily. It says *we* need to talk to them. For all we know, he followed the same steps we are now and never found anything. Maybe that's why he never told me."

"Maybe that CFK thing is a clue," Cat suggests. "I only wish we could ask him. It's so weird that he bailed after writing all this." She shakes her head. "Are you okay?"

No. "Yeah," I tell her. "But I wish I had more."

"I think *we* need to find more," Cat says pointedly. "To get to the next step."

"We?" I ask.

"Well, yeah." She sets her jaw. "You *need* me, Sam Kepler Greyson."

"And you need *me*," I say.

She laughs. "Debatable." Cat holds out her hand. "So, what do you think? Partners?"

A strange sense runs through me. It might be nausea . . . but it might also be something like hope. "Yeah," I say. "Partners."

CHAPTER
* 10 *

For the first time in a long time, I was excited to go to school the next day. I couldn't *wait* to meet up with Cat again. Unfortunately, Mom and Auddy were there to throw ice-cold water on my plan when I came downstairs for breakfast in the morning.

"Cricket, today is *test* day," Mom reminded me.

"All day," Auddy added.

That's right. Today, I have not one, not two, but *three* appointments at the cancer center. It's so many that Mom arranged an absence for me rather than trying to squeeze it around a school day. Which is why, at this moment, I'm moping in Auddy's car.

"Are you nervous?" Auddy asks me gently as she starts the engine.

"No," I say reflexively. Then, I really think about it. "Kind of."

"Just remember it's been all good news after your diagnosis," Auddy says. "You made it through chemo, and then you made it through radiation. You even kept your hair, kid."

"Mostly," I clarify. "It thinned."

"Not that much!"

"I was basically Grandpa David."

Auddy snorts. "No, Sam. You never had a comb-over. Grandpa David has a *comb-over*. Anyway, what thinned grew back. And you're strong. Everything is going the right way."

Not like with Oscar.

I'm not sure if she was thinking it, but the thought hangs in the air between us anyway. The doctors were clear with us that even though my cancer was Stage 2, the prognosis was favorable. No bulky or extranodal disease, and no B-symptoms like fevers or anything. I had a better chance of survival than anyone in Chemo Kidz—a fact that made me feel both relieved and guilty. It made me wonder if kids like me aren't supposed to be in group therapy.

Maybe we're just supposed to be grateful.

My head feels oppressively heavy as I lean against the car window, trying to ignore my thoughts. A few minutes later, we arrive at the Magnolia Center. It's a pretty name for a place that is primarily known for injecting poison into people's veins so they don't die.

"Okay, Dr. Krishnamoorthy is up first," Auddy tells me. "Then CT scan, then blood."

"I still don't get why they need my blood. Do they shake the blood vial like a Magic 8 Ball and it says 'I saw some tumors back there'?"

She smirks. "It's the CA-125. They can see certain markers in your blood that indicate the presence of a tumor."

I respond with a pointed, skeptical look that would make Gemma Monroe proud.

Auddy devastates me with side-eye. "Lord, you're a chore today. Yes, it sounds like witchcraft. But you have to do it." Auddy laughs, so I'm pretty sure she's playing. *Mostly.*

"Fine," I say, "but I can't wait until this is over and I can get back to my regularly scheduled life."

Auddy sighs. "Same, kid."

I can't help but guiltily remember my lie yesterday. But all I'm doing is trying to reset—get back to normal.

Which isn't *so* bad. Auddy just said so herself. It's what we all want.

I end up having to wait for Dr. Krishnamoorthy in the room for twenty minutes, which is annoying because we'll have to rush to the CT scan. It also means I have nothing to do except zone out and stare at the pamphlets lining the wall. Most of them say things like "Stand up to cancer!" or "Fight like a girl." The imagery shows kids karate kicking, or running marathons. As if that's something you can do when you're going through cancer treatment. Just once, I want to see a pamphlet with a picture of a tired kid on a couch.

"Lie down for cancer!"

"Nap your way to remission!"

Those are slogans I can root for.

After reading five unnecessary pamphlets, my doctor breezes into the room.

"Hello, Sam," she says warmly. "How have you been feeling? Any better now that chemo is so far behind you?"

I consider it. "I think I have more energy? Also, my appetite is better since I stopped chemo. I never felt like eating after my infusions, but then I was starving during radiation. So, yeah. I think I am feeling better."

"Great! What about after radiation? Any cough or discomfort in your chest? Skin tenderness?"

"I don't think so," I say.

"Good. Radiation can cause funky side effects even after the fact. You lucked out."

"I guess," I say with a shrug. "I mean, I was kind of hoping that I'd become Spider-Man after the radiation. But more lowkey. Maybe a chill, napping-and-peanut-butter-eating Spider-Man who fights crime in the afternoon and watches television all night."

She laughs. "I'd watch that movie. Are you feeling well otherwise?"

"Way better in the last month," I tell her. "Except for—" Dr. Krishnamoorthy's expression shifts, so I rush to add, "Just some personal stuff this month. I ate a lot of junk food."

Am I supposed to tell my oncologist that my friend died? They should stop making those weird post-cancer marathon brochures and make a different guide: *A beginner's guide to interacting with literally ANYONE after cancer.*

Fortunately, Dr. Krishnamoorthy doesn't ask me any follow-up questions. "Happens to the best of us," she says mildly. She reaches two cold hands up and onto my throat, then presses lightly up and down. It feels like she's checking for gills, but I know by now she's only looking for inflamed lymph nodes.

"Everything seems okay," she says. "Let's get you in for that CT and blood test—just to make sure. And then, I'll see you in a few months!"

After we wrap up and say goodbye, I walk out to the waiting room to find Auddy. Then, we have to more or less sprint over to the imaging center to make it on time.

We don't have to wait long before I'm called in by a pale and tired-looking lab tech. "Change your clothes, and then put everything in the plastic bag," he tells me a bit distractedly.

Nodding, I go into the dressing room and change into a needlessly complicated hospital gown with an extra sleeve. It has a set of instructions on the wall that I try to follow, but I eventually give up. When I emerge, I probably look like I can't dress myself. Nevertheless, the radiation tech has a stoic expression as he guides me inside for my scan.

Mom would call it a good "P-p-poker face" because she loves both cards and Lady Gaga. Either way, it's annoying. When techs refuse to show emotion, it sends me into a spiral in which I'm sure I have quintuple cancer.

As I'm rolled into the CT tube, I picture him talking about me later in the lunchroom.

"I just had this kid," he'd say with a sad shake of his head. "He's got three months, tops, and he doesn't even know. I'd hate to be the doctor who gives him *that* news."

Of course, this twisted fantasy leads to more unhelpful imagery—provided by none other than my nemesis, Dr. Wrongbrain. First, I see Dr. Krishnamoorthy telling Mom and Auddy the bad news as they sob uncontrollably. Then, I see Mom and Auddy standing over me in the hospital—the same way I looked down at Oscar for those two weeks. Then, they're picking out a photo for my memorial program. The details are all too real, because this is Wrongbrain's specialty. The scene plays out further and further, the thoughts fighting for room in my brain while the scan runs.

Meanwhile, of course, I have to deal with this weird whirring noise that makes me feel like I'm inside a broken air conditioner. Good times.

Ten minutes feels like an eternity, but eventually, the tech comes back in. "Your doctor will go over the results with you," he says.

"Cool," I say. "Um . . . yeah. Coolness," I add for no particular reason other than nerves.

He gives me a strange look, so I know he's capable of it, but I still can't see a trace of information on his face.

If he *had* seen a tumor, would he really be this casual?

Maybe the hospital hires androids for the radiology department. Beep-boo-beep, "Set face to: no tumor detected." Oscar moves like a cartoon robot in my mind and I snort out a laugh.

The tech gives me an even stranger look. Whatever. Ever since my breakthrough on Tuesday, I've been hearing Oscar more and more. Maybe he's winning against Wrongbrain.

That wouldn't suck.

When I get back to the waiting room, I don't see Auddy. Then I spot her outside the glass double doors, stalking back and forth and talking on her phone. I know that look. She's (very gently) letting someone have it. I collapse into one of the dated-looking chairs by the exit.

When I pull out my phone to pass the time, I immediately see a text from Cat:

Cat: Where ARE you today??? Did you get abducted by aliens? 👽

That's fair, and I wish it were true. Nerves jolt through me as I type a response.

Me: Absent today. Sorry, I'll text you later

Good. That sounds normal. Kids are absent all the time—especially since the pandemic.

"Hey, kid. What are you in for?" A voice from my

left distracts me and I put my phone down. I glance over and see a woman, who looks both elderly and tough. Her skin is paper-white but looks a little like leather. She reminds me of Grandma Gail—Auddy's mom.

"CT," I tell her. "I just finished."

"PET scan for me," she says with a stiff nod. "You okay? You don't look like you broke anything or bumped your head."

"Cancer," I say before I can think about it. Why am I telling this old lady about having cancer? Probably the whole Grandma Gail comparison. "Um, I mean I . . . *had* cancer?"

She wrinkles her brow, pressing two wild white eyebrows together in the middle. "Hmph. You don't sound so sure."

I consider my next words. "I had cancer. They're checking to make sure it's still 'had.'"

She lets out something like a snort. "That's a real stinker." Except, she doesn't say "stinker." She actually says a swear word that (1) Auddy would ground me for saying, and (2) makes me immediately grateful.

"Thank you! It is!" I exclaim. "Nobody says that. They usually tell you everything's going to be fine. Or 'You'll beat this!' You know?"

Another snort echoes through the waiting room and

98

I'm kind of psyched about how uncomfortable the other patients look. "People wanna tell you what makes *them* feel good," the woman says. "I've had cancer twice, and not one person said the right thing to me or gave me any advice I could actually use."

I catch the word. "Had?" I ask her.

She grins. "Had. At my age, they give you a scan whenever you sneeze."

I peer out the double doors. Auddy still seems to be talking on her phone. "So, what do you wish people had told you? About the cancer, I mean."

She looks up thoughtfully, and then nods with a sad smile. "I wish someone told me about the scares. Having cancer is the pits, but it's got a beginning and an end. After, though, the end doesn't feel like an end. Every shadow on an X-ray, or bump, or creak—you worry. People call you a *survivor*, and it sounds like you walked away from some plane crash. Something that's over. But it's not the same. After isn't after. It's a devil at the crossroads hunting you down."

I don't understand at least a third of what she's saying, but something feels true about it in a way that twists my insides. Suddenly I wish she would change course and tell me everything will be all right. I almost ask her to, but then Auddy stalks through the double doors.

I turn to the old woman. "Nice to meet you . . ."

"Lottie."

"I'm Sam. Nice to meet you, Lottie."

She gives me a salute with two fingers. "Same to you, Sam."

Auddy and I walk down the street to get tofu mole burritos for lunch, which usually perks me up. But I can't stop thinking about Lottie, and when I'll be able to text Cat. By the time we make it back to the medical center my feet are dragging, and I already feel like I've been drained of something. *Only one more test*, I tell myself.

"Number eighty-six, please go to station two," an AI-generated voice sounds a few minutes after we check in.

I glance down. "That's me," I tell Auddy.

"Okay, go ahead. I'll be right out here," Auddy tells me distractedly.

Her fingers are flying on her phone and I can tell she's writing an email. It's probably work. She's always busier after a holiday, and I know she had to take a day off to bring me to my appointments. Giving her a weak smile and a thumbs-up, I shuffle into the long room.

"Hello," a short woman greets me. "Have a seat."

I stick out my right arm. I know the deal.

She ties a rubber tourniquet around my arm and uses two fingers to tap the inside of my elbow. After a moment, she lowers her brow and turns my palm over, feeling around my wrist.

"You have weak veins," she huffs curtly.

I blink up at her. "Um . . . sorry?"

"I'm going to have to try your other arm." After going through the same thing on my other arm, she lets out a long-suffering sigh. "Has no one talked to you about these veins?"

"Um, no," I tell her, feeling strangely insecure all of a sudden. "One time, they had to switch arms, but nobody said anything."

"Mmm" is all the woman says as she readies the needle and scowls.

Okay, at this point I'm annoyed. I must have had a thousand blood draws in the past year. Nobody else has made me feel like my veins are flabby old losers. What is this lady's problem?

I try to convey in my expression how irritated I am, but she's already aiming the needle at my left arm. She sticks it in, her frown deepening.

"No blood," she says, taking the needle out and then trying again. The woman looks more frustrated than ever as she tries a third time on the vein near my wrist. Then, out of nowhere, an earth-rattling fart cuts through the silence.

I'll be honest. At first, I think of the tofu mole burrito and wonder if it was me. When I take a moment to assess the situation, though, I realize it wasn't. It was *her*. The phlebotomist. She shifts in her seat and another machine-gun-fire series of farts sound in the quiet room. This time, another patient peers over, snickering.

"There," the woman says.

I stare at her, unsure how to respond, and then down at my arm. Then, back up at her.

Call the National Weather Service, because that was a legit TSUNAMI of farts.

Oscar's laugh rings as clear as day in my ears. The kind that got so intense, he would end up having a coughing fit. After four vials, the woman shoos me away and I barely make it out of the door before exploding with laughter myself.

When I get to the waiting room, Auddy looks up from her phone with a smile and raises an eyebrow.

"What did I miss?"

CHAPTER
* 11 *

Mom *cannot* stop laughing about the farting phlebotomist when we tell her over dinner.

"I'm dead!" she's saying, tears of laughter streaming down her face. *"Dead!"*

Energized, I stand to re-create it for her again. "It was like this. 'Here, let me take your blood, ohhh.'" Letting out a few theatrical fart noises, I pretend to trip backward as Mom loses it.

"Oh, come on," Auddy says, giggling. "It couldn't have been that bad."

"Um, it was *worse*," I insist. "And it smelled. Like hot dogs. *Old* hot dogs."

Mom laughs so hard that I actually worry about her breathing. When she calms down enough to speak, she says, "I have one question, Sam. Was it . . . *Saw III* bad?"

Auddy looks between us. "No. Right? It couldn't have been *Saw III* bad."

Shrugging, I flash Mom a conspiratorial look. "It was close."

Back when I was in treatment, there was one really scary day. I had a high fever, and my heart started beating so fast I was afraid it would pop out of my chest. It was only a bad reaction to my first chemo drug, but we didn't know that. Mom and Auddy rushed me to the ER and we sat in the waiting room, terrified. We were all huddled together, holding hands, when a legit *blood*-curdling scream rang out. When we looked up, we saw that they were playing *Saw III* on one of the televisions against the wall. An actual *horror* movie in the waiting room. Only the three of us started to laugh—*hard*. We totally weirded out everyone else in the ER.

Mom, Auddy, and I are nostalgically recounting the tale when I suddenly remember something. *Cat.* She texted me hours ago.

"Hey, I'm gonna go upstairs and ummm . . . do some homework," I tell Mom and Auddy. Fortunately, they've moved on to another story about when Mom went into labor with me. They're too busy giggling to notice when I slip upstairs.

Guilt eats at me, in spite of the fact that I'm not *lying*, per se. I might talk to Cat about the California History Project, which is homework. And yeah, a tiny part of me is still feeling guilty for not telling them about the note. But Cat told me herself that hardly anyone believed Kevin's lie. So, it's a nonissue. At least, I hope it is.

When I get upstairs and check my phone, I see three texts:

Cat: Okay, but definitely text me. I did ALL the research!

Cat: Now I'm worried. Are you sick?

Cat: I stopped by the library on the way home but you're not there either. Seriously, are you okay?

Oof. That's impossible to answer.

I take a deep breath. How am I supposed to respond? I scramble to think of a good answer that *isn't* oncology or a farting phlebotomist.

Me: Ack, sorry! I forgot to tell you. It's Yom Kippur, so that's why I was absent. You can tell me all about your research tomorrow, right?

I press send and immediately panic. It was the first fall Jewish holiday I thought of, but now I remember that there's a whole other holiday before Yom Kippur. Rosh Hashanah. *Mom so hasn't prepared me to lie about*

Jewish holidays. This is really a failing on her part.

Cat: . . .

The dots seem to dance for a thousand years. Finally, a response pops up.

Cat: Isn't Yom Kippur weeks away? Rosh Hashanah is first, right?

What? How does Cat know that? Our school is so lazy about acknowledging Jewish holidays. Not that we celebrate either. Auddy makes latkes for Hanukkah and we do a humanist Haggadah for us to read at Passover Seder. But those are the only holidays we celebrate. Auddy never officially converted, in part because Mom is, to quote, "a highly skeptical agnostic." She never even had a bat mitzvah.

I don't know *how* I feel yet. I used to keep kosher with Auddy, but everything fell apart after my diagnosis. This spring, I brought home a bunch of Levain Bien sourdough rounds, gave Auddy my best sadboy eyes, and said "But I have *cancer.*"

Cat: I just googled it. It's weeks away.

Cat: Gia's best friend is Jewish so I know.

Ah! She won't give up. And is she a spy? Who notices that kind of thing? I text her back the most fact-stuffed lie I can think of.

Sam: Oh, yeah, I meant both Rosh Hashanah and Yom Kippur. My extended family is here, and this is the only day they're in town. So, we decided to unofficially celebrate now. We had matzo brei for breakfast (my favorite) and then hung out with them all day today. We had noodle kugel for dinner.

I let out a breath of relief, hoping that my bizarre amount of detail will make her stop asking questions. At least I wasn't lying about my love of matzo brei. That stuff's good.

Cat: Ok cool.

Whew! I make a mental note that any future deceit should be a little harder to fact-check.

Sam: Anyway, I didn't have time to do any research. Well, except I did look up the transcript for that open hearing Congress had about unidentified aerial phenomena last year. Did you read that?

Cat: Of course. But that's not why I was looking for you. I think I found RC Fitzwilliam!

Sam: Really?

Cat: Well I found R.C. Fitzwilliam the author at least. He wrote a bunch of articles for this online news zine called *The Daily Skeptic*. Nothing for a while and he doesn't seem like a believer, but still interesting stuff. How many

R.C. Fitzwilliams could there be who ALSO write about UFOs? It has to be the same person.

Sam: Nice! Wanna talk about it when we meet up next week?

Cat: Or we could meet up tomorrow? I know it's the weekend, but we could go to the library again if you're free. I have plans with Leslie and Zooey for lunch at the mall, but I can meet you after. Like 3?

Sam: See you then. I'm gonna go watch Otherworld bc of course I am (⌐■_■)

Cat: Nice! What episode are you on?

Sam: Venatrix

Cat: The one with the Italian shape-shifting witch hunters?

Sam: Yep, the Benandanti. I'd hate for those ladies to be after me.

Cat: Because you're a witch?

Sam: True facts.

Cat: Hahaha, makes sense. Ok, 'night!

I blink at my phone. It's so weird that I'm texting Cat Pellegrini now. I don't know, maybe it's only research. But it's almost like a . . . friend thing?

Before I can get in my head about it, I decide to look up *The Daily Skeptic*. It doesn't take me long to find R.C. Fitzwilliam.

Huh. Cat was right. It looks like Fitzwilliam hasn't written anything in a while, but a quick check of the archive shows articles from 2002 until 2013. When I start reading from the beginning, I see why he was a good fit for *The Daily Skeptic*. The headlines read:

"Another UFO Myth Busted."

"Circular Object Proved to Be a Ham Radio Balloon."

I love Gemma Monroe's healthy sense of skepticism, but this guy sounds like he's dead-set on proving UFOs don't exist at all. *Definitely* not a believer. How did he end up as a moderator on a site that publishes firsthand UFO accounts?

After an hour of scanning the articles, I grunt in frustration. There's nothing—at least, nothing that points me toward Oscar or the symbol. Is it possible that the name Oscar wrote down in our book *isn't* linked to the symbol? Yesterday, I thought for sure it was the connection I was looking for, but maybe I was wrong. And why can't I find *one* UFO site with that image?

Oscar's voice floats into my mind on cue. *It's connected, Sam. You know it is.*

"Since you can talk to me now, some more specifics would be nice," I grumble.

I decide to try one more thing—an advanced search with the words "Fitzwilliam" and "UFO." Then, I narrow the search to dates between 2002 and 2013. A few results pop up about finding your ancestry, and the Fitzwilliam coat of arms, but then I see it—a link that reads: "Why I Changed My Mind About Unidentified Aerial Phenomena" by R.C. Fitzwilliam.

I click on the link and make a loud noise when the next screen pops up. It goes right to *The Daily Skeptic*, but a little broken computer face pops up with the error message "Something went wrong, please check the URL and try again."

"Aghh!" I groan, closing the tab. After taking a few seconds to feel sorry for myself, I reopen the search bar, typing in the name of the article verbatim with narrower date parameters. Right away, something pops up. An old thread from an inactive subreddit called r/UFOBelievers.

Posted by **u/eve7&8** 10 yrs. ago
Found this in *The Daily Skeptic* but it disappeared. I only got a screenshot of the headline and 1st few lines to send to my buddy. The rest of it was behind a box that said "click to subscribe." Anyone see those? I thought internet news was free, but I guess the 1% is making sure to cut off our access until we pay. When I checked

```
back it had a broken link. If they scrubbed
it, it can't be good. I think the article was
from 6 months ago. Anyone else seen this?
I bet he has something.
```

No replies to the post, and only a handful of upvotes. Holding my breath, I look at the screenshot, then I read the headline again and the opening lines.

```
    For years, I had a mission: to prove
that the "unexplained" wasn't so unex-
plainable. That was two weeks ago. Then,
everything changed with one simple piece
of evidence I could have never—
```

Maddeningly, the screenshot cuts off there, in the middle of a sentence. After years of writing articles debunking UFO accounts, why would he change his mind after meeting one abductee? I read the Redditor's last words again: *I bet he has something.*

Did R.C. Fitzwilliam take the article down himself, or was it removed?

And did Oscar find the whole article somehow? I don't know. We usually did our own research between seeing each other. He must have found *something*. Right?

I close my laptop screen, my mind swirling with possibilities. There has to be a *reason* that R.C. Fitzwilliam changed his mind after years of being a skeptic.

And I can't escape the feeling that Oscar wants me to find it.

CHAPTER
* 12 *

By the time I get to the Rose Garden Library the next day, Cat is already waiting for me with the same precariously stacked pile of ancient books.

"Oh, good, you're here!" she says hurriedly, moving a bunch of papers around and organizing the books into stacks.

It gives me time to notice Cat's weekend clothes. She looks different than she usually does at school. Her hair, which is usually down and neatly wavy, is up in a haphazard bun. Instead of jeans, she's wearing leggings and an oversize long-sleeve tee that shows the phases of the moon. She doesn't look like a carbon copy of Leslie or Zooey. It's . . . nice.

"Hey," I say, sitting and dropping my bag on the table.

"Hey," she replies distractedly. "So, after you texted

me about the article last night, I kept looking. I didn't find anything new, sorry. I also couldn't find an email or phone number for R.C. Fitzwilliam. I guess let's just DM him through his Foo Fighters profile and hope he responds. Even if he doesn't know about the symbol, maybe he can point us in the right direction." She lets out a sigh.

"I saw a phone number for the editor in chief of *The Daily Skeptic*," I offer. "May be a long shot, but we can call him to see if he has a hard copy. Or, if not that, contact info for Fitzwilliam. We can DM him, too, but it's good to cover our bases, right?"

"Yes! Let's call him, too!" Cat says it loud enough that a few library patrons look up from their books and computer screens.

I lower my own voice and peer around the library. "Maybe not here, though."

Cat winces. "Yeah. How long are you free today? My parents have a church get-together, so if we wait until five we can call from my house. That way it'll be quiet, and my parents won't overhear and ask a bunch of questions." Her eyes move back and forth rapidly, as if she's trying to keep the schedule straight.

"That's cool," I say carefully, swallowing a question about what would happen if her parents overheard. "In the meantime, we can get some work done on the history project."

Cat laughs. "You mean, the project we should actually be working on? Yes. Oh, by the way, have you interviewed your mom yet? You said she was here in 1989, right?"

"Not officially."

"I haven't sat down with my mom, either," Cat tells me. "She was here for it, but Dad was still in Chile. Let's work on some interview questions, so we're ready to get pr—"

"Primary sources," I interject with a snort. "I know."

She frowns. "What's wrong with primary sources?"

Smirking, I say, "Nothing. You've just made it clear you love them. I look forward to the joyous day that you become Mrs. Primary Sources."

"Shut up!" Cat says, but she giggles so I know I didn't go too far. "Besides, I wouldn't take 'Sources' as a last name."

I sweep my hand dramatically. "Mrs. Catalina . . . *Sources*."

Cat kicks me under the table.

"You're Mr . . . um . . . Gemma Monroe."

I cross my arms, smirking. "Not an insult."

"Mr. Always Wears Hoodies?"

"You are so bad at this."

"Your . . . *face* is bad at this."

I roll my eyes and put on a slow clap. "Well done."

"Aghh! Whatever!" She smiles while she kicks me again.

We spend the next hour and a half coming up with interview questions, and making a Loma Prieta timeline.

Cat taps a pencil against her cheek thoughtfully as we finish up. "Man. I can't even imagine what that was like."

"What?" I ask.

She shivers. "You know. These people waited hours or even *days* to find out if the people they loved were alive or not. And then having to tell the story later, for books like this. How did anyone remember specifics when the world was crashing down around them?"

7:16 p.m. That's the exact time the phone rang and Mrs. Padilla told Auddy.

I shrug off a full-body shiver.

Dr. Wrongbrain sends me flashes of images and feelings from the night we found out. Squeezing my eyes shut, I silently ask Oscar to make it stop.

Hey, check it out. I . . . AM . . . NO . . . MAN!

Oscar waves around a giant sword in my mind, wearing his favorite Pikachu pajama pants. He sweeps it to one side triumphantly, as if to cut down Dr. Wrongbrain.

Get it? I'm totally Éowyn killing the Witch-king of Angmar. Which is a little confusing because I also want to marry Éowyn.

I can feel myself start to smile.

"I'm sorry, what is with your face right now?" Cat asks, folding her arms.

In an instant, I remember that we're talking about earthquake fatalities and I'm grinning like some kind of ghoul.

"Sorry," I mumble. "My mind just wandered to . . . something I heard."

I hold my breath, wondering if she's about to bolt and write me off as a jerk. Fortunately, she only raises one eyebrow and shrugs, apparently letting it go. That's the second weirdo reaction I've had around Cat. Maybe I need to cool it with my Oscar thing when she's around.

"Whatever," she says. "Let's go. It's almost five and we've got a Fitzwilliam to find."

"And . . . go," I whisper, pointing at Cat after a long beep sounds. A half hour later, we're back in Cat's room and leaving a message for the editor of *The Daily Skeptic*.

"Hello, this is a message for Mr. Lippi," Cat says in a low-toned voice. "My name is Cat and I'm a student at the University of San Francisco. I'm trying to track down an article that you posted in 2013 by one of your staff writers, R.C. Fitzwilliam. I'm hoping to get a copy of the article for a source and possibly interview Mr. Fitzwilliam for a thesis I'm working on. If you could give me a call back and let me know how I could contact him, that would be greatly appreciated." Cat rattles off her number at the end and hangs up the phone.

"Very nice," I say, clapping. "You sounded old."

"Thanks," Cat says, laughing and pretending to swat me with her phone.

We'd decided before making the call that Cat would pretend to be a college student.

"People don't take teenagers seriously," Cat pointed out, "and definitely not thirteen-year-olds." She isn't wrong. I always get treated like a little kid when I'm with Mom and Auddy. But lately, if I walk into a store without them, I get these guarded looks that make me feel weird.

"Okay, so now that we're done with the call, I also wanted to show you a few more articles about EQLs before my parents get home," Cat tells me, grabbing her laptop.

"Oooh, new ones?" I ask excitedly.

"Ones you haven't seen, at least," she says. "I don't

think I ever showed you the full article from *Science on the Fringe*. You know, the one from that first day at the library?"

When she says the name of the journal, my excitement deflates a bit. It apparently shows on my face, because Cat frowns when she notices my expression. "What?"

I sigh. How do I say this? "The thing is, *Science on the Fringe* isn't . . . *reliable*."

Great, Sam. You win at tact.

Cat looks offended. "All right, *Gemma*."

"A compliment!" I reply in a singsong voice to lighten the mood, but it only deepens her scowl. "Sorry," I tell her after a second. "All I meant is: if we're looking for evidence that we can use, we should draw from sources that can't be questioned."

"That's fair," she says. "In that case, there's another *site* I want to show you—a blog with anonymous first-hand accounts. Who knows? Maybe R.C. Fitzwilliam is a mod there too."

I scoot closer as she points at her laptop screen. The banner reads: *Citizens of the First Kind*. "What does that mean?" I ask. "It sounds familiar."

"See, that's the problem with your Gemma-skepticism," Cat says with a smug grin. "You miss out on things. Does Hynek's scale sound familiar?"

I wrack my brain. "Maybe? Yeah, actually, it does. Remind me."

She leans forward eagerly. "There was this astronomer, J. Allen Hynek. After the Roswell incident, there were tons of reported UFO sightings. The government—military, I think—hired this Hynek guy. They couldn't tell which of the reports were planes, or weather balloons, or whatever. So, they asked him to sort out the accounts that might be a threat. Hynek developed a scale that measures the severity of close encounters: of the first, second, and third kind."

"Whoa," I say, impressed. Cat's knowledge of this is *next* level. "What's the first kind?"

Cat scrolls around for a moment and then nods. "It means you saw a UFO, but it didn't have any physical impact on you or the stuff around you—that would be the second kind. And, obviously, you don't have direct contact with an extraterrestrial life-form."

"The third kind," I finish her thought. "Does it go past three?"

"Not on Hynek's scale, no. But there's a few authors in *Science on the Fringe* who have claimed that other types exist, and the military is trying to hide something." She looks sheepish. "I know a lot of this stuff is silly. And probably made up. But I find it interesting."

"Hey, I find it interesting too," I promise.

Cat drops her gaze, fidgeting with her hands. She suddenly looks so uncomfortable and preoccupied that I want to make her smile again.

"Have you ever heard of a close encounter of the twelfth kind?" I ask.

She peers at me. "What? That's not a thing."

I give her a sage look. "Oh, it is. It's when the aliens come down in their UFO and bring you a Taco Bell Crunchwrap Supreme."

Cat bursts out laughing, and I feel a rush of pride. She tilts her laptop screen so I can see the whole page without arching my neck. "Let's see what we can find," she says.

"It looks like the blogs and comment threads go back more than five years," I murmur. "But look. They cover all the unexplained sightings from the last twenty years. The trucker sightings in Jersey, the USS *Nimitz*, and, look, here's one in New Mexico from a few years ago. It might take a while to—" I stop short, grabbing Cat's laptop.

"Hey!" she protests.

I can't believe what I'm seeing. Under the blog marked "USS *Nimitz* UFO Sighting," I see a comment from a user named baskoskervilleisl.

Anyone out there know when they're releasing the UFO report? I need to know for sure if they're out there, or if we're totally alone in the universe ¯_(xx)_/¯

Below it is a reply from a user named R0wanc@Fitzwllllam:

anne reeta wool

What could that mean?

"Sam . . . what is it?" Cat is asking me. "You're freaking me out."

I move to show her the screen again. "I think this reply is from R.C. Fitzwilliam. And the person asking the question . . . it's Oscar."

CHAPTER
* 13 *

"*C FK!*" I exclaim, facepalming. "How could I not see that right away? Oscar wrote 'Tell Sam we need to talk to RC Fitzwilliam at CFK.' *Citizens of the First Kind*."

"Whoa, wait, this is really your ex-friend?" Cat says, peering at the comment. "And R.C. Fitzwilliam responded? Why wouldn't he tell you that?"

Because he died before he could.

"I have no idea," I lie through my teeth.

"Well, that's it," Cat says. "If we don't hear back from Fitzwilliam, we have to ask him. What if he knows something we haven't found yet? Look, if you don't want to, maybe *I* could be the one to call Oscar. I still don't get why he would write that in the margins like he planned on telling you, and then unfriend you like that. So weird."

My throat scratches as I swallow a bad taste. I'm wracking my brain, trying to think of how to somehow invent an Oscar with a different last name that she'll never find. This lie is literally the *worst*. When I lie about feeling okay, at least, I don't have to make up any more elaborate stories.

I know what I need to do. I *need* to tell her the truth. Summoning all of my bravery, I open my mouth to set Cat straight.

"Oh, wait!" she yells before I can say a word. "This site has profiles, just like the Foo Fighters site. Do you think Oscar went to his personal profile and contacted him off the thread? If so, we could message R.C. Fitzwilliam here. And Oscar, too."

I let out a relieved sigh, but I *should* tell Cat anyway. Right? So why, whenever I picture telling her, do I keep seeing Kevin's face?

When I told Kevin I had cancer last May, he got this *look*. His eyes immediately shot down, like he couldn't bear to look at me. He shuffled his feet and then legit *backed away*. It was maybe ten seconds before he mumbled some excuse and disappeared. The thought of Cat's face dropping like that—of her suddenly treating me like something to get away from . . .

The image immediately grows and spreads like a tumor in my chest. Not my lazy, slow tumor. An aggressive one.

Because it's Cat. She isn't one of my online Rocket League friends, or some random from school. It's *Cat*. I close my eyes.

"Sam!" I hear Cat saying. "Earth to Sam!"

"Sorry," I manage to croak out. "Um, we could message Oscar . . ."

Because, why not? It's not like Mr. and Mrs. Padilla are taking over Oscar's obscure paranormal internet profiles.

But . . . oh god, what if they *did*?

"But he's obviously given all that up," I rush to say. The lie comes out without any effort, but guilt stabs at me. "And I'm not sure Oscar will know any better. His note said to 'keep looking,' right? Sounds like he never actually found anything solid. That's why we need to finish what he started. Besides, the response to his question here was . . . nonsense."

"That's a word for it," Cat mutters. She seems too distracted to notice that I'm just rambling excuses at this point, which I'm grateful for.

"It's better if we contact R.C. Fitzwilliam directly," I add for good measure. Staring at the screen, I repeat the strange message. "*'Anne reeta wool.'* What does it mean?"

Cat turns back to her laptop. "Maybe it's a company name? A fabric company—wool?"

"Why would R.C. Fitzwilliam tell Oscar the name of a fabric company?" I point out.

"I don't know," Cat murmurs. "But it doesn't matter. These search results are nonsense too. There's no company with that name."

I stare at the words and they seem to lift off the screen, jumbling around. It feels like when Auddy and I do one of our crazy-big puzzles and I start to see the pieces come together in one big picture. The noise in my brain—Cat, the lie, Kevin, and Oscar—suddenly fade far enough into the background for me to focus. When I do, something snaps into place. "Wait."

"What is it?" Cat asks eagerly.

I clumsily reach for a pen from her desk. "Paper," I say. I'm afraid that if I don't get this down, it might disappear.

She reaches into her bag and hands me a quiz dated from last week. "Use the back," she tells me when I stare at it a beat too long.

I nod, writing down the words.

anne reeta wool

Then, I start to pull out letters.

an ret o *alone*

an ret o *we alone*

"What are you doing?" Cat asks, knitting her brow.

"I think it's an anagram," I tell her without looking up.

a re *we not alone*

WE ARE NOT ALONE

I hold the paper up triumphantly. "Look! *We are not alone.*"

"Whoa!" Cat says, her eyes lighting up. "I'm impressed. I've always been terrible at anagrams. But why would he answer in code to begin with? Seems . . . paranoid."

"I don't know," I say. "But what if we message him the anagram and solution? We could say we're looking for information for . . ." I trail off. "Adult reasons?"

She snorts. "Yes, let's message this man again and say we're looking for information for *adult reasons.* That will make us seem all grown up."

I throw up my hands dramatically. "Okay, what's your suggestion?"

Cat laughs. "I actually agree. I'm just teasing. So, we DM him on both sites with the same message we left for

The Daily Skeptic—which we were going to do anyway. But, then we add a few specifics *and* quote this anagram to see if he bites?"

"That might work! Hopefully he checks regularly."

"Should I ask about the symbol?" she asks. "Or do we want to get him talking first?"

I pause, considering it. "We don't know for sure that he was the author of that newsletter. And he might just tell us we've got the wrong guy. Don't mention the symbol yet."

"But don't we want him to be interested enough to write back?"

"The decoded response should do that. If we don't hear back, we'll send the symbol."

"Okay!" Cat says. She focuses on her computer screen, typing furiously for a minute or so before looking up with a triumphant smile. "Done! Want to read before I send?"

I lean over and scan her message. Under the decoded message, she'd written:

Mr. Fitzwilliam,
My name is Cat, and I'm obtaining my degree
in geophysics. I've read your work in The Daily
Skeptic *and I'd love to interview you for a research*

*project I'm doing on theoretical studies pertaining
to unidentified aerial phenomena. Please respond
as soon as possible.*

"It's perfect," I say. "Send it."

An hour later, I find myself back home, alone. Mom and Auddy are out on their weekly dinner date, which means I'll be feasting on my favorite meal: every cereal in our cupboard, mixed together. It's an art form, learning how much of each cereal to add, but I've mastered it. Tonight, it's Major Munch's "Oops, All Chocolate!" O's, Cake Flakes, and Honey's Oat Clusters.

The house feels empty and a little spooky as I finish my cereal. The bowl makes an ominous clatter that echoes throughout the house, and a shiver runs through me from head to toe.

"Calm down," I mutter to myself as I head upstairs. Mom and Auddy will be back by nine at the latest, but I feel like I need to create some noise to drown out the heavy silence. When I get upstairs, I quickly change into pajamas and put on *Otherworld*.

As Gemma flashes across the screen, I can't help but think about Cat.

For one, I still can't believe she's annoyed by the one,

the *only* Gemma Monroe. How can she be, when the whole skeptic thing is literally the reason Baskerville is alive right now? He would still be trapped in ice in the Caves of Tamaid if it weren't for her, and that's the truth.

For another, Cat's eyes are just like Gemma's—hazel, but with these cool gold flecks. Or am I imagining things? I pull out my phone, instinctively looking for a picture, like I would of Auddy or my mom. But, of course, I don't have any pictures. There's literally zero proof that Cat and I are even friends. Minimizing my photos, I take a deep breath and install Instagram.

Mom told me that social media has gotten scary—especially in the past few years. But it can't hurt to make a fake account. Oscar had one. His "finsta." I smile as I remember the profile picture he used—it was his favorite lucha libre wrestler, Rey Mysterio.

I decide to take a page out of Oscar's book, making a profile with a picture of my favorite monster from *Otherworld*. Before too long, I find Cat's profile and see that it's private. I need to request to follow her. *Pass.* I'm just about to put my phone away, when a loud beep sounds.

"Ahh!" I cry out when I see the notification.

Cat: Nothing yet. Do you think I should tell R.C. we'll pay him one billion dollars?

It's Cat, and I find myself immediately tensing up as if she can see me trying to look at her profile. I quickly go to the settings of my fake account and press delete.

"Yes, delete!" I yell at my phone. "I'm sure I want to permanently delete!" Finally, my fake profile icon disappears. Dear lord, I'm a dork. And I am *never* joining social media again. That was traumatizing. Letting out a nervous laugh, I go back to my texts.

Sam: Don't think that guy gets out of bed for less than a trillion.

Cat: Aw man, I only have a billion. That's out.

Cat: Are you watching Otherworld?

Sam: Do you even have to ask? Code Orange.

Cat: A classic. Any suggestions for me?

My breathing starts to relax and I even smile. I don't know what I was freaking out about before, but I blame Instagram. And I have the perfect answer for Cat.

Sam: Clach'mheallain. You're welcome.

Cat: Ohhh, the pterodactyl people. YES. Okay, you served your purpose, you can go ;P

Cat: 'Night, Sam.

Sam: 'Night.

I press play again and, as the opening credits roll, I can't stop smiling. It could be the fact that this is the episode where Gemma Monroe makes her funniest faces. Or the fact that the ambient musical score seriously calms me down.

I can think of another reason you're smiling, Oscar whispers at me.

"Whatever, man," I say. "You don't know what you're talking about."

Remember when the Krysa Virus is released in that Russian prison and Baskerville got it? And what he said to Gemma in the hospital? That she was his BEST friend.

That dude just loves to tease me. Still, is Oscar right? Are we actually becoming *friends?*

"Sam!" Auddy's voice floats up from downstairs. "We're home. Is someone over?"

"Um, I'm up!" I yell, flushing as if they could hear my thoughts. "Hold on!"

This is ridiculous. It's only been like five days. Cat and I can't be *real* friends. Maybe we're friend*ly,* but it's less a friendship and more of a . . . temporary ally-ship.

Yes. That makes the most sense.

But, as I push off my covers and head downstairs to see Mom and Auddy, I can't help but escape the feeling that I just told another lie.

CHAPTER
* 14 *

Monday morning starts with yelling, but not in a bad way.

"Sam! Breakfast!" Mom calls out just as I roll over and hide my face in the pillow.

"Uggghhh," I moan, even though they probably can't hear me.

"I have to work early and you have to eat breakfast. No Pop-Tarts!" Mom barks.

"I'm making orange challah French to-oooast!" Auddy calls out after her.

My mouth starts to water from merely hearing those four magical words. *"What?!"*

I clamber downstairs as fast as humanly possible. Usually, I need a minute or two to wake up, but *hello!* This is Auddy's orange challah French toast. That's a special circumstance. When I get downstairs, I suck it down in thirty seconds flat.

I'm full and happy when I get into the car with Auddy—and surprised to find myself *not* bummed about going to school. Most days, I'd be happier avoiding human interactions and instead watching TV all day. But, today, I'm dying to know if Cat heard back from either of her messages—from *The Daily Skeptic* editor or R.C. Fitzwilliam. I find myself imagining all the possible replies we might have gotten when Auddy's soft voice breaks in.

"Penny for your thoughts."

"No thoughts here." I swipe a hand up and down my body. "Only French toast."

"If you say so," Auddy replies in that knowing voice of hers. "Only, I noticed you were more preoccupied than usual yesterday. And that was during an *Otherworld* marathon. Usually, I can't get you to pry your eyes away if Gemma Monroe is on the screen. You tend to *swoon*."

My face heats up. "I wasn't preoccupied. And besides, I'm not the only one who swoons. Mom has heart eyes for James Baskerville, we all know it."

Auddy laughs. "Well, yes. That's true."

"Are you jealous?" I ask with a wicked look.

"Are *you* trying to change the subject?" Auddy

counters. "Because you've only made me curious as to why you're avoiding the topic. Or *who* could be interesting enough to distract you." She puts a hand up to her temple in mock contemplation.

"You're imagining things," I mumble.

She offers me a serene smile. "If you say so."

I try my best to hide my blush, but fail miserably. Maybe I should just tell Mom and Auddy I've been hanging out with Cat. Then Auddy would let go of whatever theory she has, and she and Mom could stop worrying about the whole "Sam is a loser with zero friends" issue. Before I can really consider the idea, however, we pull up at school.

The bell rings just as I'm sliding into my morning class—pre-algebra. After coasting through my first two classes, I head to the school library for my free period. Auddy had arranged for it months ago because I was still in radiation at the time and we didn't know what my scans would look like after treatment. I conveniently forgot to bring it up when I started last week and my evil scheme worked—because here I am, *not* having to run a mile on a muddy day. Muhahaha.

I'm busy staring at my old checkered slip-on shoes as I walk to the library. I've just rounded the corner when I slam into someone.

"Hey!" an annoyed voice sounds. I look up to see Nathan Briones scowling. "Way to be *burgundy*."

"Sorry," I mutter. Before he can react, I duck past him and into the library. One of these days, I might actually snap and demand to know what "burgundy" means. But today is not that day.

If only those cancer commercials could see you now. So brave.

"Ha ha," I say aloud, rolling my eyes. "Sick burn, Oscar."

"Are you talking to me?" a voice asks from my right. I spin around, embarrassed when I see Ms. Huynh shelving books in the nonfiction section.

"Um . . . yeah," I say, flushing. I'm already a liar, and allegedly burgundy. I really can't add "The boy who talks to himself" to the list. "Just looking for you to see if you need any help."

"I'd love the help, but don't you have anything to work on today?" she asks.

"Not really."

"What about the California History Project?" Ms. Huynh asks, little beeps sounding as she checks in a pile of books.

"My partner and I are ahead of schedule," I tell her. "We drew the 1989 earthquake."

The beeping stops, and Ms. Huynh looks at me. "Oh." Her face holds a familiar expression I can't quite place. "I was actually living in San Francisco at the time. We . . . unfortunately lost someone."

Now, I know that expression. It's the same thing I see in the mirror every morning after I wake up and Oscar isn't there. Tired, and maybe a little bit haunted.

"I'm really sorry I brought it up," I fumble.

"No, it's okay, Sam," she says, the haunted look passing. "It was a long time ago. In fact, if you're looking for someone to interview, I'm happy to talk about it. I talked to another pair of students five or so years ago."

"That would be great!" I say in a strangely excited tone. What is *wrong* with me?

Ms. Huynh smiles. "Just let me know what day you and your partner want to come in."

I thank her, heading to the nonfiction stacks. Why was that so hard for *me*? What is it about Big Things™ that makes everyone completely malfunction? I can't tell if we're all terrified of saying the wrong thing, or that people think bad luck is contagious.

Whatever it is, even I'm not immune.

Shaking it off, I head for the tables near the fiction stacks. I end up getting ahead on a few assignments during my free period. When the bell rings, I head to the cafeteria. It's lunch, which means I can track down Cat and we can finally talk in person.

It's not long before I see her, sitting with her head facing away and chatting with Zooey. I feel a nervous tingle, but try to appear confident as I walk toward the table.

I clear my throat once I'm behind them. "Hey, Cat?"

Not one head turns my way, but I am being quiet in a loud cafeteria. I try again.

"Cat?"

"Oh, hey!" Cat says with surprise. She doesn't say it in a mean way, but I still feel like I'm suddenly in my underwear in public.

I'm just opening my mouth to tell her about our interviewing Ms. Huynh when a rough arm slumps around my shoulders.

"What's up, stalker?" Kevin laughs, and his breath is hot in my ear.

I let out a disbelieving scoff. "What?"

Leslie gives me a dark look as she sidesteps around me and sits at the table with Cat. I guess they all eat together now.

"Stalker says *what?*" Kevin says. He's still laughing, but his tone has an edge. "But seriously, you're always hanging around Cat. It's weird. Are you trying to make her feel sorry for you or something?"

"Kevin," Zooey says. "Come on. Stop it." Her voice is firm.

"Why? What did I say that wasn't true?"

Literally everything, Kevin, I think. First, he tells people I lied about having cancer, and I'm a *stalker* now? I know it was mostly about gaming, but I seriously can't believe I was ever friends with this guy.

My blood boiling, I reach up and push his arm off my shoulders. It falls to Kevin's side like a limp noodle, which only makes him laugh harder.

"We're paired on the project," I seethe, looking at Cat to confirm, but she doesn't meet my eyes. Instead, she looks down nervously.

Mortification washes over me.

For the first time since I got back to school, I look Kevin in the face. I'm hoping that, as soon as I do, it'll be over. I can hate him as much as he clearly hates me. But as soon as I look at him, my heart sinks to my feet. I glance back at Cat, but her head is still down.

"I have to go," I say, turning away.

"Bye, stalker!"

All I can hear is Kevin's laughter echoing behind me as I walk out the door.

CHAPTER
* 15 *

A thousand emotions surge through me like fast-acting poison. But, in reality, it's only one. The sadness I felt as soon as I looked at Kevin's face is . . . overwhelming. All I can think of are three words, on repeat.

I miss Oscar.

I miss Oscar.

Because I do. I miss my friend.

I head for the only safe space I can think of—the same bathroom I'd hidden in on the first day of school. I lock myself in a stall, reaching into my backpack. I've had Oscar's memorial program neatly tucked inside since that day—when I hid from the crowds, trying to decode his last message. I'd taken it with me in case I wanted to see his face.

I *need* to see it now.

Slowly, I unfold the program and look down. Oscar's picture looks so odd and unlike him. He's younger and pre-chemo, but it's not just that. His eyes are bored and his hair is combed and slicked down. His expression is one only I could read as *Take the hecking picture and get me out of here.*

"Come on, Oscar. Say something," I beg him. "Tell me how to get out of this."

There's only silence, save for my wet sniffles and my feet tapping nervously against the cold tile of the bathroom. Because, duh, Oscar isn't even *real*. He's in my head.

Then, my mind flashes to Cat. Is *she* even real? All of a sudden, I worry that I need to file this whole maybe-friendship in James Baskerville's famous box of "unsolved occurrences."

When the bell rings, I'm not sure what to do next. My feet feel as heavy as lead, and my head is throbbing. There's also the fact that my next class literally has Kevin, Leslie, Zooey, *and* Cat. How am I supposed to be in class with all four of them after what happened at lunch?

I can't.

As in, I *really* can't.

With all of my effort, I make my way toward the

door and out into the hallway. Students move and hum around me until it all sounds like white noise. Then, I see it.

The exit.

There's no teacher stationed there, or a security guard. What's to stop me from just . . . leaving? I've never cut school before, but I'm afraid I'll die if I walk into that classroom.

Before I realize it, I'm through the door and halfway down to the parking lot.

As I make my way farther from the building, my mind races. Auddy works from home today. I always expected to walk home with Cat after the library, but I can't see her. Maybe I can go to the library until three. If I leave then, Cat won't find me. Then, I can go home, put on *Otherworld*, and Auddy will never . . .

Wait.

The school. They'll call Mom and Auddy.

I struggle to think of a good excuse why I left school in the middle of the day, but my head is too crowded. The lies have multiplied and tangled into each other—and now I can't see which one works for which person.

With my mind racing, it takes forever to get far enough away from school that I'm out of sight. A weird tingle at my chest suddenly makes me blink and look down, where I'm surprised to find my hand. It's rhythmically scratching at my chest, where my shirt hides the sad-worm chemo scar. Oof. Moving your hand without your brain even knowing it can't be a good sign.

Deep breaths, Sam.

I consider reaching into my bag and taking out Oscar's memorial program again. But, just as my fingers close around the glossy pages, I finally hear his voice.

It's not any more interesting the hundredth time around. "Oscar *was a good little boy who loved his family and God and NEVER ate junk food or stared longingly at pictures of Zendaya.*" Blah, blah, blah . . .

I smile ever so slightly as his image becomes clearer.

You know, you can just tell them it was about me.

"What?" I murmur aloud.

Just tell them that's why you left. They won't ask questions.

That's true. It's not as if Mom and Auddy wouldn't understand. If they find out, it won't be the end of the world.

Slowly, my breath calms and my muscles loosen. After another few minutes, I make my way to the library. One foot in front of the other. By the time I get there, I feel almost . . . relaxed. Right away, I find a chair and sit, taking my favorite paperback out of my backpack and starting to read. At first, it's impossible to focus, but finally I find myself sucked in, barely looking up until a voice sounds above my seat.

"Sam?"

Cat is standing over me.

Well, great. My heartbeat ratchets back up immediately, and I'm surprised to find that what I'm feeling most right now isn't sadness—or even fear of being embarrassed again.

It's anger.

"Go away," I mutter, grimacing as I look back down at my book.

"Sam," she says softly.

"What are you doing here anyway?" I point at the clock, which reads 1:55. Then, I put on a voice I reserve for when I'm *really* irritated—Auddy calls it *Sam*casm. "Shouldn't you be in history class by now with all your bestest friends?"

"I got a bathroom pass when I didn't see you in class," Cat explains. "Then, I just . . . left." She fiddles with a chunk of her hair, then flips it behind her shoulder.

Unable to help myself, I ask, "What *is* that?"

She flinches. "What?"

"The hair flipping. You do it constantly."

"I mean, I see other girls do it," she protests.

"And, what? You're a robot studying human behavior? Are you Data from *Star Trek*?"

Her expression drops. "Data's an android, not a robot."

"Well, I guess that answers my question about whether you were lying to me about being a nerd," I say with a snort.

She frowns. "Why would I lie to you about being a nerd?"

I fold my arms. "I don't know what to think. We've been hanging out and texting for days but suddenly you act like you don't even know me. I mean, Kevin called me a stalker in front of everyone. Even Zooey told him to stop. You didn't. *You* barely even looked at me!"

My voice rises instinctively with every word until I see a few heads pop up, looking at us curiously.

Lowering my voice, I add, "So what am I *supposed* to think, other than that you've been messing with me?"

"I know. I froze, but that's no excuse," Cat says sadly. "But I came to say sorry, okay?"

"Why would you say sorry?" I say with high-key Samcasm. "Apparently, I'm *stalking* you. Right?"

"Sam . . ."

Crossing my arms, I say, "How am I supposed to believe that after today? Cat, you just sat there while he treated me like some kind of creepy . . . *freak*." I know I'm being a little harsh, when Cat didn't say anything bad about me. But she also didn't *say* anything.

Cat looks stricken. She buries her face in her hands and, after a second, I hear whimpering. Oh, man. Is she crying? Did I take it too far?

I have no idea what to do with a crying person. I mean, *I* cry. Pretty much constantly. At the oncologist; when Baskerville talks about his missing mother in *Otherworld*. And, you know, *Moana*. But Oscar was surprisingly stoic, and my moms always retreat to their room to cry.

I've got zero real-world experience here.

"Um, it's okay," I say, awkwardly patting her back.

Cat looks up and her face is red and streaked with tears, her hair plastered to her cheeks. "It's really not. You're right, Sam. He was so mean to you and I did nothing." She laughs, but the sound is sad and hollow. "Which is basically *me* being mean to you. *You*. As in, the only person who's let me be *myself* for my whole life. And I messed it up."

Yeah, you kinda did, I think. But even I know that's not fair. I wish she'd said something, but that doesn't make it her fault that I miss Oscar, or that Kevin is such a jerk.

"Look," I say tentatively. "I was only so mad because . . . ah, never mind."

"What?" Cat asks. She blinks at me hopefully.

"Because I thought we were becoming friends, okay?" I blurt. "A few days ago, it seemed like we had so much in common. And I *never* find someone who I have stuff in common with. Except . . ." I trail off again, his name freezing in my throat.

"Sam. We *are* friends," Cat says. Her voice is thick with tears as she adds, "You might be the best friend I've had in my whole life, and I only found you a week ago."

My traitor heart swells with hope, but I try to ignore it. "But you said it yourself. You pretend to be someone else at school. How are we supposed to be friends when I'll never know who I'm getting?"

She stares at her feet.

I facepalm. "I don't get it. What is so awful that you have to hide who you are?"

"It's not awful, but . . ." Cat shakes her head. "Look, you don't know. If I tell you, you'll think *I'm* a freak. And then you'll leave, and then Mom and Dad will know, and then—"

Suddenly, looking at Cat is like holding up a mirror. Maybe she's worried about telling me something because she can see the game board too. Every bad possibility, every darkest timeline.

"Cat. You can tell me," I say. "I promise I won't go anywhere."

Then, Cat blurts out the last words I expect to hear.

"I saw one, okay! That video I said I saw on YouTube in fifth grade. The earthquake. It was me. *I'm* the one who saw a UFO that night."

CHAPTER
* 16 *

At first, I sit there, unable to respond. She saw a UFO? As in, an *actual* real, live UFO?

"Sam," Cat says anxiously.

"Uhhhhhh."

Just form words, Sam. There is no wrong response here, but it has to include *words*.

"*You're* the guy from YouTube?"

Okay, that was the wrong response.

For a second, Cat just looks confused. Then, she looks around and says, "There never was a guy from the internet. It was me. *Me*."

I hate that my first reaction is to ask her if she's *sure* she saw a UFO. "Ummmm—"

"Oh my god," she mumbles after I don't go on. "You

don't believe me. I can't—"

"Wait!" I say. "You just caught me off guard. *Please* tell me."

Her face clouds over, but she doesn't leave. "Okay," she stage-whispers, her eyes darting around. "But . . . outside."

I grab my backpack and follow her out the double doors to a small garden alongside the parking lot. Once we get to a bench, Cat slumps down, motioning for me to sit next to her. "You have to promise you're not going to laugh at me. Or tell your moms. Because they'll tell my parents I told the story again and they *can't* know."

I sit, taking a deep breath and reciting the one line I know will convince her to talk to me. "I promise, Agent Monroe," I tell her in a British accent. "Broken promises die in the starlight, but mine will shine forever."

Cat flushes red. "You did Baskerville."

"I did," I reply, probably twice as red as she is. "And I don't do that lightly. My moms tease me. *Mercilessly.* So. Do you believe me now?"

"Okay." Cat takes a deep breath. "It was right after my great-grandma's funeral."

"I'm sorry," I interject softly.

"Thanks," she says, her expression strained. "It

was . . . complicated. Great-Grandma Marie was always kind of mean to me. She pinched my midsection and asked what my parents were feeding me. And she always said I looked sloppy. Whatever that meant."

"Oof," I say. "That's not awesome."

"It wasn't. Anyway, my mom wanted me to say something at the burial. Gia spoke, and so did my mom and dad. But I just couldn't bring myself to lie. So, I snuck away. I ran off into that tunnel of trees I told you about." She glances at me, as if to make sure I really want her to keep going.

"And after that?" I prompt.

Cat sighs. "After that, everything I told you was true, only for me—the earthquake, the lights, everything. Everyone at the service felt the earthquake, but somehow nobody saw what I did. The lights were big and bright enough that at least dozens of people should have seen it, though. I still can't understand it."

I lean back against the back of the bench. "Wow," is all I can say.

"Yeah. So, that experience jump-started my alien obsession. Big surprise, I know."

"Did you tell your parents?" I ask. "Is that why . . . you're always so worried about them knowing what you're doing?"

"I didn't tell them at first." Cat's shoulders slump. "They started asking questions when they began seeing signs of my new hobby. Then, I told them the truth."

"And?"

"Well, you know, what you'd expect. They said I was making it up. They forced me to go to therapy, and then asked the doctor if I needed to be on medication for hallucinating." She lets out a humorless laugh. "I guess I wasn't the kid they ordered."

"Which was what? Someone who mega-hearts nail polish?" I try a light joke and it works. Cat looks back at me with a weak smile and touches her finger to her nose.

"Yeah. I don't know. They probably wanted someone more like Gia."

I raise my arm to put it around her comfortingly, but then awkwardly pull it back, knocking my backpack off of the bench. Of course, the zipper is undone, so a bunch of papers and books dump out onto the dirt. It's not the first but the *second* backpack explosion in a week. Do I have a problem with zippers?

"And now I made you drop your stuff," Cat mutters, helping me as I scramble to pick everything up. "I'm—"

She breaks off, and I look up.

"Oscar Padilla, 2011 to 2023," she reads aloud.

My heart drops. She's holding Oscar's memorial program.

The moment before she looks up from the program feels like a thousand years. I can't even hear the street noise around us. All I hear is my own heartbeat, beating at triple speed. I open my mouth twice to speak, or head this off at the pass—*anything*. But I can't figure out how to start. Finally, Cat raises her eyes to mine.

"He didn't ghost you. Your friend . . . died?" she chokes out.

"Yeah," I croak.

Okay, now is the time to tell her everything. There's no going back. She'll ask what Oscar died of, and I'll tell her. And then she'll ask how I knew him. Half the truth is out already; I need to just fill in the rest.

"Oh, Sam," Cat says. "I'm so sorry." She rests a hand on my shoulder. "And I was so pushy about contacting him. I feel *terrible*."

Oh, man.

"C-Cat," I stutter. "There's something else I need to tell you—" The words die in my throat, and dread hits me in the gut.

Suddenly, her face blurs, and I see Kevin. But . . . *no*. This isn't about him.

Cat *is* my friend. Who just told me something incredibly private. She trusted me enough to tell me something even her best friends don't know. I can't keep this from her anymore.

Dr. Wrongbrain fills in the worst thought: *You thought Kevin was your friend too.*

All of a sudden, it's like I'm an actual game piece, the board spread out in front of me. Which way do I move?

"Actually, he died of cancer. I have cancer too."

Move five spaces to the Orchid Center. Dr. Krishnamoorthy says the cancer is back.

No. That's ridiculous. Saying it out loud won't bring my cancer back. But it won't get me any closer to getting my life back, either. I know exactly what I need to do, but—

"Sam? Do you want to tell me something?" Cat's voice floats in, sounding worried.

My words betray me before I can stop them. "It's nothing."

I can practically see Oscar facepalming.

Nothing?

It wasn't a huge lie, I tell myself. "It's nothing" could mean I don't want to talk about it. Is it really so different from the lies I tell Mom and Auddy—my "I'm fine!" moments?

But . . . no.

I can't justify this. Those lies are for their sake. This lie is different. It wasn't for Cat. It was for *me*.

And now I don't think I can take it back.

CHAPTER
* 17 *

"Tell me about Oscar," Cat says softly as we walk toward her house a few minutes later. When I don't reply right away, she stares at the sidewalk. "I mean, if you want. I don't mean to push."

I spot a rock on the sidewalk and kick it off to the side. "It's okay. It doesn't always make me sad to talk about him. Sometimes, it even makes me happy."

Cat glances over at me. "But it happened pretty recently, right? The program had a date."

"A month ago. It took time to plan the s-service." It hurts a little to get the words out, but I manage. Still, I hate how much my voice is cracking.

"I'm sure you miss him," Cat says.

"I do."

"Gah," Cat groans, "this *sucks*. I'm so sorry you had to go through this."

I'm not the one who died, I almost say. I mean, it did happen to me, but it still feels strange to frame it that way.

"Thanks for saying it sucks," I tell her. "That's the best way to describe it."

"You don't have to talk about him right now," Cat says. "If you don't want to."

"He loved Nintendo," I tell her quickly. I'd rather talk about Oscar than stay stuck thinking about my terrible decision-making.

"Yeah?"

"Yeah. We got through nearly every game. Mom saved some of her old consoles, so we even played Mario Three and Diddy Kong Racing—you know, the oldies."

"I don't know Nintendo well," Cat admits. "But isn't it Donkey Kong?"

"There *is* a Donkey Kong, but this game is Diddy," I correct her.

Cat cocks her head. "The rapper?"

"No, Diddy *Kong*."

"Oh. Is he, like, Donkey Kong's son?"

"Nephew," I clarify. "Well, it depends on which guide you read. I'll catch you up."

She grins, but then her expression immediately crumbles. I know that look.

"It's okay to smile, you know," I offer. "And laugh. I do it all the time, even when I'm sad." To prove it, I give her a silly look. "Oscar was a goof too."

Cat smiles, and it sticks this time. "Did Oscar like *Otherworld*?"

"He did! I introduced him to it—that's actually why we started our *Guide to Finding Intelligent Life*." I'm starting to hit my limit on talking about Oscar—any more and I'm afraid Dr. Wrongbrain will enter the chat. "Hey, do you want to watch *Otherworld* when we get back to your place?" I ask, hoping that will naturally break up the conversation.

It works.

Cat's eyes light up. "Um, always! My parents won't be home until at least five, and I should probably introduce you anyway."

"Because we're *friends*, right?" I keep my voice light, but inside I need her to confirm it.

"Sam," Cat says, holding my gaze. "I meant what I said before. I only hope I can be half the friend you've been to me."

Relaxing, I say, "Okay."

She clasps her hands together. "Really? Because I'll

even learn Donkey—I mean, *Diddy* Kong racing, if that's what it takes."

I tent my hands maniacally like that was my plan all along, and she laughs.

When we get to Cat's house, we head to her room. Immediately, Cat shrugs off her backpack and pulls out her phone.

"Oh yeah," Cat laughs, looking down at it. "I totally forgot to turn this back on after I ditched school." She abruptly freezes, turning back to me with a horrified expression. "Oh my god. I ditched *school*."

"We both did," I point out.

"But I *never* do stuff like this. And there's no way my parents aren't going to find out. I left in the middle of class, Sam! They are going to *freak*. As in, they'll probably start checking my phone every night."

Now she's starting to get me nervous. I pull my phone out of my pocket. No new messages. Okay. So, Mom and Auddy don't know . . . yet. But I know I'll have to face them later.

"What if you told your parents that you spent the rest of the period in the bathroom throwing up?" I suggest. "You could say that you bailed as soon as the bell rang."

"Wait, that's good!" she says, giving me an approving

look. "If I didn't know you're not *actually* a liar, I would think you were pretty good at this."

"Um, yeah," I say with a nervous laugh.

Bling bling-bling! BLING bling-bling!

A trilling sound comes from Cat's phone.

Cat immediately spirals. "Do you think it's a message from the school? Are they telling me I'm a truant? Are they sending the same message to my parents? Oh god, oh, god. I'm totally getting shipped back to St. Chris. They'll make me do catechism."

"Okay, do you still want to introduce me?" I ask. "Because it sounds like your parents *are* strict, between how freaked out you are and the Christmas-decorations thing."

She blinks. "What 'Christmas-decorations thing'?"

Oops. It's like my mouth is actually malfunctioning, lying when I shouldn't and telling the truth when it's the worst idea ever. What's next? I blurt out that Auddy's nickname for Cat's mom is the Merry Mussolini?

"Uh . . ." I hedge. Then I opt for redirection. "Dude, check your phone! Get ahead of it."

"Okay," Cat says nervously. She presses her screen and gasps. "It's not the school. I got a private message from R.C. Fitzwilliam! It's on my Citizens of the First Kind account."

"Open it!" I urge her.

Grinning, she clicks the notification and peers at her screen, reading the message aloud:

"November Alpha Mike Echo Oscar Foxtrot Uniform Sierra Alpha India Romeo Foxtrot Oscar Romeo Charlie Echo Sierra Tango Uniform Delta Yankee Oscar November Uniform Foxtrot Oscar Sierra One Nine Five Two . . ." She trails off after rambling out the long string of words. "Um . . . *huh?*"

I groan. "Wow. There isn't even an introduction, or response to the rest of our message? Just another code?" Frowning, I reread the string of words, and this time, my mind snags on something. *Oscar. Alpha. Echo . . .*

"Wait. I know this," I say.

Cat looks at me with surprise. "You do? How?"

"I . . . don't know. Hold on." Quickly, I pick up my phone and type a few of the words into a search box. As soon as I add "Tango" and "Foxtrot," the code comes up. "Yes! This is it," I say. "It's the NATO phonetic alphabet. Oscar thought it was hilarious that his name was in the code."

Cat gives me a sly look. "Such nerds," she says, shaking her head and smiling.

"Says the nerd," I scoff.

"Fair," she confirms. "Okay, so we just need to spell

it out and give R.C. Fitzwilliam a response. That's not so hard. Or I hope it won't be."

I scrawl the words as their corresponding letters until I've written it all. "N A M E O F U S A I R F O R C E S T U D Y O N U F O S." I recite. "Then one, nine, five, two. 'Name of USA Irf . . .' no."

"'Name of US Air Force'?" Cat suggests.

"Yes! 'Name of US Air Force Study on UFOs.' The last words are numbers, so . . ."

"1952," Cat mumbles, looking thoughtful. "So, a study done by the Air Force in 1952."

"Wait, do we just send this back, or do we need to look it up?"

"Probably look it up. That part should be easy . . ." Cat says, trailing off. After a few seconds on her phone, her eyes light up again. "Okay, I think I've got it. Project Blue Book."

"Don't they mention that on *Otherworld*?" I ask. "I swear it was in the episode where Baskerville and Monroe—"

"Found the hybrid alien warehouse!" Cat finishes my sentence. "It was. Also, remember when I told you about the Hynek scale?"

"Yeah."

"Look! *He* was the advisor for Project Blue Book!

Doesn't it feel like everything is falling into place?" She lurches forward and envelops me in a hug.

Every part of me screams *Danger! Girl contact!* but I try to ignore the impulse to pull away. Oscar wasn't a big hugger, but this is what friends do, right? Right?!

I take a few seconds longer to compose myself than I would have liked, and ask, "So we have a message to send back, right? Do we ask about anything else, like the newsletter or the symbol?"

I shake my head, answering my own question. "If he's responding in code, it feels like he's testing us. Until we pass whatever test this guy has in mind, I don't think he'll answer any questions."

"That's true. I only hope he writes back faster this time. Do you think he will?" Cat's sparkling eyes hold on mine and I instinctively look away.

First a hug, and now direct eye contact? Way too much.

When I glance to the right of Cat, I end up catching sight of the time and my stomach sinks. Five fifteen. "Oh no!" I yell. "I told my moms I'd be home by five."

Cat follows my gaze. "Um, I'd say you're not going to make it. Not unless you have the Tempus Polyhedron." She giggles at her own *Otherworld* reference.

As Cat rushes me downstairs, we hear the front door

open with a *click*. A gray-haired man in a button-down walks in, stopping with surprise when he sees us.

"Hello, *cuore mio*," he says, beaming at her. His smile falters ever so slightly when his gaze falls on me. "I didn't know you had . . . company."

"Sorry, Dad," Cat says quickly. "This is Sam. He's my partner for the California History Project. I meant to introduce you last week, but you and Mom were out late. Anyway, he has to get home."

"Nice to meet you, um . . . sir," I say awkwardly as Cat ushers me out the door.

"Nice to meet you, Sam," I hear him call out.

"Sir?" she scoffs as soon as we're outside. "Dork."

I can feel myself blushing, so I make a joke to cover it. "That's Mr. Dork to you."

"All right, *Mr.* Dork."

"Oh, hey, what does '*cuore mio*' mean?" I ask as I sling my backpack over my shoulder.

Cat smiles, blushing. "It means 'my heart.' I don't remember if I told you, but my dad is from Chile."

"Is it Spanish?"

"No, Italian. Dad's actually Italian-Chilean. It's more common than you think."

"Cool. My moms call me 'Cricket.'" The minute it's out of my mouth, I almost facepalm.

Why, Sam?

Cat responds with a sly look. "Well, you're gonna have to tell me about *that* tomorrow."

"We'll see," I say, smirking and turning toward the street.

"Later!" she calls after me. "I'll text you if we hear back from R.C.!"

I wave goodbye to Cat, hit by another wave of guilt as I recall my lie from earlier. During my quick walk home, I find myself replaying the day's events. Maybe I can find a way to reset. If I can only find a way to tell Cat the truth that *wouldn't* end in disaster . . .

I'm so busy internally role-playing the scene in full that I don't see Mom sitting on the porch as I walk up the street to our house. When I finally catch sight of her halfway up the path, I stop dead in my tracks.

"Sam Kepler GREYSON," Mom's voice booms. She waves her phone at me in a way I immediately understand is about more than my being late. Mom's eyes blaze, fiery enough to melt me into a puddle of lava.

"You," she hisses, "are in *so* much trouble."

CHAPTER
* 18 *

There was no other option, except to tell them about Cat. The partial truth I'd prepared about missing Oscar wouldn't cut it after I stayed at Cat's past five. Once they got home from work, all bets were off.

Of course, I'm not remotely ready to tell the full "I lied to Cat about not having cancer" truth. Or the "we're breaking a series of codes from some guy on the internet" truth. But I'm hoping that telling Mom and Auddy about my new, honest-to-goodness friendship might save me a two-year grounding.

"So, that's it," I say, after the end of my long explanation. "Cat and I had a fight and I just got so upset about missing Oscar that I *bailed*. I couldn't let anyone see me that way. Then, Cat found me at the library and we made up and lost track of time."

I watch Mom and Auddy trade a stone-faced look, but I can tell they're budging. And it's at least three-quarters of the truth.

"I'm so sorry," I say for the fifth time. "I'll never do it again, I promise. But, so you don't worry, I went right to the library, and then to Cat's house. I didn't go anywhere weird, or ride on a motorcycle, or drink beer and drive our car into an Arby's. You know, like that guy we saw on the news last week? So . . . silver lining."

"I told you we shouldn't let him stay up for the eleven o'clock news," Auddy huffs.

"Audrey, we're raising a boy. A *boy*. And a progressive. He needs to be aware of what's going on in the world. And about the consequences of bad behavior."

Auddy rolls her eyes. "And making sure he knows about the dangers of drinking and driving into an Arby's is step one."

"We both know it was some guy who thought he was entitled to a free Meat Mountain value meal," Mom insists, waving her hand. "Survey says *patriarchy*."

Auddy doesn't even say anything. She just gives Mom her most disbelieving-lawyer look. This is great. Maybe they'll end up arguing about Arby's and the patriarchy and forget about Cat.

Mom turns back to me. "So, tell us about Cat! Is she

nice? A good student? Does she have red hair like a certain MI-6 agent?" Mom's eyebrows threaten to wiggle right off her face.

Okay, maybe not.

"Mom, it's not like that," I moan, feeling my face heat up. "We're just friends, okay?"

Auddy puts a finger to her chin thoughtfully. "As long as she's nice, that's what matters. I'm just glad you're making new friends."

"Oooh, what about their names?" Mom trills.

Uncharacteristically, Auddy's eyes light up. "Sam and Cat. Cat and Sam. So cute!"

Sweet mother of dragons, what have I *done*?

"MOMS! This is not a girlfriend situation! We're friends. *Friends*." I flail my arms in a dramatic show of disapproval, but Mom just grabs my hand and stares at Auddy.

"Sam and Cat!" Mom sings, clapping her hands for each word. "It sounds like a high-end clothing brand for babies, don't you think, Audrey?"

A high-end clothing brand for BABIES. Oscar is more vivid than ever in my mind, wheezing out the words as he laughs his butt off.

Dude, you two are so precious.

I shouldn't be surprised that he'd side with them.

Any excuse to mock me. I close my eyes, but I can still hear them talking. Also, closing my eyes doesn't block out the image of Oscar straight-up cackling at me.

Rising from the couch, I heave a sigh and say, "Well, I'm gonna take off."

"No, no, no!" Mom and Auddy shout in unison.

"We'll be good," Auddy says. "But you're going to have to talk to Principal Romero tomorrow. And Ms. Wong, and apologize to them both. Okay?"

"Okay," I say, letting out a nervous breath. "But . . . are *we* okay? Are you still mad?"

They exchange a long look that seems to hold a thousand words. After a beat, Mom nods and Auddy turns to me.

"We're okay . . . this time," Auddy says. "Because you told us the truth."

I swallow hard, the actual truth so close I feel like I might have to cram it back down my throat. Although a big part of me wants to get it over with and spill everything to them, I keep my mouth shut through dinner and our nightly television hour. Because they seem so happy for me. And also just . . . *happy*. Giggly, even.

I wonder what would happen if they knew it all. What happened today with Kevin would make Mom blow through the roof, but the lie I told Cat is the one that would really change things. Mom and Auddy wouldn't be giggling and teasing me. They would just be sad.

I'm tired of making them sad.

By the time I head upstairs to my room, I'm so tired I think I might pass out.

"Sam?" a voice sounds from behind me as soon as I'm through my door.

I turn to see Auddy, who wears a knowing look along with her smart pantsuit. She stops at the doorway.

"Did I forget to put my dishes away?" I ask.

"Nope. I only wanted to tell you I'm proud of you."

Closing my eyes, I feel a flash of sharp pain. It goes away for a moment, but then comes back throbbing, settling deep in my chest. I move to sit on the bed so she doesn't notice. I'm almost afraid to open my eyes again, so I keep them shut as I ask her, "Why are you proud of me? I totally messed up today."

"You did," she says, moving to sit down next to me, "but you also went through something really terrible a few weeks ago. And you've been . . . scarily well-adjusted about it. Maybe I'm a little proud of you for messing up. Relieved, at least."

Still unable to look at her, I bury my face in my hands. "I don't feel well-adjusted."

It's true. Even though I knew it was likely that Oscar

wouldn't make it, there was a big part of me that was sure he would. Not because I thought his treatment was working, or because of some deep-down faith.

I thought he'd live because . . . how could *Oscar* die?

What sense did that make? Being mad at the universe isn't all that satisfying, though. It doesn't get mad back, or do some kind of evil cackle when it messes with you. It just . . . *is*.

"You don't have to be well-adjusted," Auddy tells me in that soft and incredibly level voice of hers. "Not a lot of kids have been through what you have. You're two kinds of survivors, Sam. All within this year. But that doesn't mean you have to act well-adjusted or *lucky* or thankful. You get to feel the way you feel."

She looks right at me, and I don't even try to stop myself. My chest clenches up as I let out five full minutes of sobs, letting myself lean into Auddy and feel the comfort of her arms around me. It's basically a cry-po-calypse. Way worse than when Moana sees that spirit manta ray and knows it's her grandma. Of course, now that I'm thinking about Moana's grandma, I cry even harder.

"It's okay, Sam," Auddy says, hugging me tighter.

"But it's not," I say in a thick, snotty voice. "It's not okay, and it's not fair."

"Well, yes. But, Sam. It's *okay* to say it sucks."

I let out a sharp laugh that almost hurts. "Don't let Mom hear you say 'sucks.' She'll never stop teasing you. It's not 'proper language.'" I put on my best "high society" face.

Auddy grins wickedly. "Cancer sucks. Sucks, sucks, SUCKS! If it had a face, I'd punch it. Also, it *sucks*."

She holds my gaze, and then both of us erupt into a cascade of laughter that feels good.

"You feeling better?" she asks.

"Yeah," I tell her. "But . . . tired. I think I just want to put on *Otherworld* and fall asleep."

She winks from the doorway. "Good choice. Say hi to Baskerville and Monroe for me."

"Auddy?"

"Yeah?"

"I love you. *So* much. Maybe I don't say it enough." More tears threaten to escape but I go on anyway. "I'm glad you picked Mom."

Auddy walks over and plants a kiss on my head. "I picked you, too. Best decision of my life, kiddo."

She pulls me in for a long hug and we stay like that for another minute before I tell her I'm ready to go to bed. Somehow, I manage to watch her leave my room without crying all over again. I spend a few minutes sitting there, thinking about everything Auddy said about how I don't have to act like a survivor even though I am one. After a while, though, my head feels heavy. I've only just put on pajamas and crawled into bed when I hear a melodic *ping* from my phone. I smile when I see Cat's name pop up on the screen.

Cat: The vomit story totally worked! My parents even gave me frozen yogurt for dinner because I said I couldn't imagine eating whole food. What about you?

Sam: I have to talk to the principal and Ms. Wong tomorrow. Can't run, can't hide from Mom and Auddy. They were nice though.

Cat: Boo about Principal Romero. But the second part reminds me, did you interview your mom about the earthquake?

Sam: I did on Sunday, I forgot to tell you. It's a good story, but I think if we want to ace, we need something better. Ms. Huynh said she'd talk to us, and her family knew someone who died in the earthquake.

Cat: Oh wow, that's great!

Cat: NO! I mean, how horrible and tragic!

Cat: I'm a terrible person.

I laugh aloud at this one, going for my best Samcastic response.

Sam: It's okay. You just love primary sources more than

you care about people. I'm sure Ms. Huynh will understand.

Cat: YOU'RE THE WORST.

Sam: I know I'm the best.

Cat: The WORST

Sam: And smart and beautiful? Well, now you're going too far.

Cat: I did NOT

Sam: Please, I have to stop you. I'm flattered, but I've been spoken for. By Gemma Monroe.

Cat: Okay I'm gonna go plot your murder.

Sam: Have fun!

Cat: Ugh. Good NIGHT.

Sam: Best wishes.

Cat: AAAHHH!!! I'm done with you now.

I'm just about to respond, when I get another text from Cat.

Cat: Wait, Sam . . .

I see the little typing dots bobbing up and down, until I finally get a new text, and a loading image.

Cat: HE WROTE BACK!

When the image loads, I see a screenshot of the familiar light green text on black background I recognize from the Citizens of the First Kind page. I read the message and sigh.

It's another weird clue, because of course it is.

BHIIA Xcnnglq Uvtggv (19.6.20 B 6.23.4, E 2.3.11)

My mind races. I have . . . no idea what this means.

Cat: I think the middle part might be a reverse alphabet cipher? But I have no idea about the part in parentheses, or the other ones.

Staring at my *Otherworld* poster, I silently ask for help from Baskerville and Monroe.

"You got anything for me, Oscar?" I mumble under my breath, reading the email again.

You got me. It looks like an alien language.

I can't help but wonder if Oscar did break the Anne Reeta Wool code. If so, what did R.C. Fitzwilliam say to him? Did he have to solve a bunch of puzzles too? I inhale deeply and write back to Cat.

Sam: We've got a lot of work to do.

CHAPTER
∗ 19 ∗

Cat and I spend the next week in obsession mode.

R.C. Fitzwilliam's message appeared in my dreams every night, swirling around and mixing itself up. Oscar was getting quieter with my mind occupied, although at times I could almost feel him peering over my shoulder curiously as I studied the nonsensical code.

Cat and I tried the reverse alphabet decoder, but it didn't make any sense when we translated it. Since there were numbers, we also tried to decode it using the A1Z26 cipher. It's what it sounds like: a code that translates letters into numbers based on their place in the alphabet. A=1, B=2, and so on. From that, we got a possible number—28991.

Using that same code on the numbers in the parentheses, we also got the word "shift" and the number two.

Which only got us to:

28991 XcnnglqUvtggvUJ (sft2fwd4bck)

Still total nonsense.

By the time Monday rolled around, we were getting desperate.

I had a moment where I *almost* considered going over to talk to Mr. and Mrs. Padilla and asking them if I could see Oscar's room. Because a question still ebbed at me: How much did Oscar actually know?

I talked myself out of it every time, though, because I'm so not ready to see the Padillas. How would I be around them? Too sad, and then they would have to comfort me? Or maybe I wouldn't be sad enough. What if they thought that Oscar dying was no big deal to me? The idea made my stomach turn.

Today, after another hour of staring at the code after school at Cat's house, both of us are ready to give up.

"This is making my brain hurt," Cat complains. "Time for a TV break." She pushes a pile of papers away from her and groans in frustration.

"If it's *Otherworld*, can we watch 'Baskerville versus the Hounds'?" I ask, propping a pillow behind me on Cat's bed. "It's basically the best episode of all time."

Cat gives me a dramatic clap. "Congratulations on being so tragically wrong."

I raise a hand to my chest in mock offense. "You wound me, madame," I say, putting on a vaguely snooty British voice. "I'm *always* right."

"The best episode is 'Big Blue,'" she says matter-of-factly.

I scoff. "I mean, that one is *fine*. But it's a schlocky monster of the week."

"The Monster of the Week episodes are the *best* ones," Cat argues. "But, fine. I actually like 'Baskerville versus the Hounds.' I'll watch it if you promise we'll watch 'Big Blue' next time." Cat turns on her TV and sits next to me.

"Fine." I hand Cat her stuffed alien. "You gonna need Jorge? This might get scary."

Cat smacks me over the head with Jorge. "Shut up!"

She cues up the episode, and soon I see the familiar chaos of James Baskerville's office. There's this giant wooden desk with an ancient-looking astrolabe and mixed-up papers here and there. On the shelves are a hodgepodge of strange contraptions that look like they're from the 1800s. I love that we never find out what they do. Then, there's the quintessential element: a blown-up grainy image of a UFO that Baskerville himself had taken.

"Monroe, my dear, I think you've been cursed with my company too long," Cat speaks aloud with the show.

"Have to agree with you there," I reply in a breathy Gemma voice. "The most disturbing part is that it seems to be rubbing off on me."

Cat throws back her head and laughs.

We go back to just watching but, after a moment, Cat pauses the episode and gives me a scrutinizing look.

"Okay, I have to ask you something," she says, leaning in a bit.

"Um, yeah?" I reply nervously. For some reason, I'm suddenly very aware of how close she's sitting.

Is this weird? I think about Oscar and me, sitting on his bed and playing Link's Crossbow Training. That was never weird. . . .

"Do you think that Baskerville and Monroe kissed that night for real?" Cat blurts out her question excitedly before I go too far down my spiral. "You know, the one where they travel back in time to World War Two?"

At this, I manage to relax and let out a snort. "I don't think any of the stuff in the time-travel episodes really happens, so no."

This wasn't the answer she was expecting. "Wait. What?"

"Well, they travel back in time to prevent that *other* time traveler from going back to kill Hitler because killing him was going to lead to some *mecha*-Hitler, right?"

She frowns. "Yeah?"

"But they *theoretically* change the whole thread to that future. I mean, I guess there could be a future in which they fail to stop the Hitler-killer and come back to the present. But, at that point, they could be returning to a future where mecha-Hitler changed everything. That's why I don't like time travel when it's not a *whole story* about time travel."

I swear, I'm only saying regular words, but each one seems to enrage her more. "But if they *hadn't*, then Emperor Kimbot would have totally destroyed Earth!" she protests.

Oscar and I used to fight about this stuff *all* the time. But Cat's different, and it's as if my brain finally catches up to that fact. "Sure," I say. "Emperor Kimbot would have been bad. If that time traveler had stolen the Enigma machine and brought it back to the future . . ." I trail off, wincing at Cat's expression. "Ummm. I mean, I don't know, maybe they did get together. The show leaves it pretty vague."

I think I said *close* to the right thing, but she still scoots away from me, an odd look on her face. Were we actually talking about *Otherworld* right then? Now I'm not so sure.

See, this is why I hate time-travel episodes.

I pick up the remote, about to un-pause the episode, when she speaks up again.

"The Enigma machine," she murmurs.

"Wait, what?"

Suddenly, she stares at me, wide-eyed. "Sam! The Enigma machine!"

"You're just repeating the words!" I say, throwing my hands up. "You need to actually explain them."

She scoots all the way off the bed and rushes to her desk, riffling through the papers. Then, she grabs a pencil and starts writing.

I drop the remote. "Cat. What is it?"

"Ever since R.C. Fitzwilliam sent us the NATO phonetic code, we've been studying cipher styles, right?" she asks.

"Yes . . ."

"Playfair, AutoKey, Morse, and SHiFT codes that can be decrypted using a key and a machine like the Enigma."

"I see where you're headed," I say gently. "But even if it's that kind of code, we don't have the key." I let out a huff. "Maybe R.C. Fitzwilliam did it on purpose—sending us an unsolvable code."

Cat holds up a finger as she writes down the code again. After a few seconds, she looks up at me triumphantly.

My skin breaks out in goosebumps. She found something. "What is it, Cat?"

"We've been running in circles all week, trying to think of a decryption that would fit this exactly. But what if it *was* a changing cipher, like that Caesar one we read about. For a code like that, we would only need to shift to get the answer, as long as we had *directions*."

I stare down at the code. "S, F, T. F . . . W . . . D, 4 B . . . wait, Cat!" My eyes pop. *"Shift two forward, four back!"*

Cat grins at me triumphantly. "Sam. We had the key all along!"

CHAPTER
* 20 *

Once we have the key, it only takes a few minutes of trial and error.

"And J . . . shift two forward, four back and . . . got it!" I yell, writing down the full message. "So, 'Xcnnglq' . . . whatever, is really Vallejo Street, SF."

"28991 Vallejo Street, SF," Cat says, leaning back. "So, San Francisco."

"Do you think it's where he lives?" I ask. Then, I pop my eyes out. "Or maybe some government warehouse that has every piece of evidence we need?"

Cat laughs. "I think if he had that, we'd be seeing more UFO coverage on the news. Maybe it's a meeting place? At least San Francisco isn't far. But we don't know when."

I type the address into the search bar of my maps

app and look at her with a shrug. "What if we just went there?"

Cat frowns. "How would we get there?"

"I don't know. BART? The bus?"

"My parents would ask why," she says, looking at me meaningfully.

"And that would be bad," I finish the thought.

"Yeah. It would be bad." Cat's eyes flit back and forth and I feel like I'm looking in a mirror again, wondering if she's considering all the ways it could go wrong. Of course, this is the first time in over a day I remember my lie, which sends guilt washing over me again.

One of the benefits of obsessing over this code 24-7 has been how distracting it is. There are times that this feels like my real life now—me and Cat solving a puzzle like normal kids. Which, for these brief moments, make me forget I had (have?) cancer at all. It's in those moments that, no matter how guilty I feel, I end up keeping the truth inside again.

Just a little longer, I keep telling myself.

"Sam?" Cat breaks in with a searching look. "You went quiet. Are you in there?"

"Yeah, sorry," I say. "I zoned out. What were you saying?"

"I was only saying that, as much as I want to find

R.C. Fitzwilliam and ask him what he said in that article, we're still guessing that he has something solid. And I'm not willing to take a bus to some random location without knowing more. You know?"

I sigh. "Yeah."

"We've waited this long," Cat says. "Why don't we email R.C. the solution? He got back to us pretty quickly after we solved the NATO one."

"You're right," I say. "Maybe he'll get back to us with a plan."

Cat and I spend a few minutes drafting a simple message to go along with the solution that asks a few questions about the location, and whether this means he's agreeing to an interview. After we send it to R.C. Fitzwilliam, Cat turns the show back on and we wait.

We don't need to wait long. By the time the credits roll on "Baskerville vs. the Hounds," a notification rings. Cat rushes to check but, when she does, she only lets out an exaggerated groan.

Huffing, she shows me. "Another code."

⌐⌐∧□⊓Ⴑ∨□⊓> 23

"What the what?" I moan. "This is even harder than the last one!"

Cat doesn't speak, the skin between her eyebrows creasing curiously. She traces the bottom row with her fingers. I scoot over toward her, peering at the message. Is she seeing something that I'm not?

"Aaaahhh!" she yells finally, tossing her phone down. "It looks familiar but I can't place it. My brain hurts."

"It looks familiar to me too," I say. "Hey, you've been doing a lot of the cipher research. Why don't we call it for now, and you let me take a crack at it this time? You can get our questions ready for Ms. Huynh's interview tomorrow. Deal?"

"Deal," Cat says, tossing down her pen. After a second, she looks up at me and a smile breaks out across her face.

"Sam?"

"Yeah?"

"I just wanted to say . . . it's been really nice being myself these past few weeks."

"It's been nice getting to know . . . yourself," I say, laughing.

"You're the best," Cat says. Something about the words make me feel both happy and a little disappointed, but I don't have time to figure out why. Before I can react, she throws her arms around me in a huge bear hug. By today's count, she's hugged me eight times.

I still can't quite get used to it, but this time there's a new problem.

"Ow!" I cry out instinctively as a loud crack sounds from my sternum.

Cat pulls back and I'm once again hit with a strange wave of disappointment. She winces, looking at me with concern. "Omigod, I'm sorry. I didn't think that would hurt you."

"It didn't. Not really," I say. "I swear." But my chest, which now blooms with a dull, spreading ache, doesn't agree. I rub it inconspicuously.

A pain never feels like *just* a pain now. I think about the starting point of that horrible game. When Auddy took me to the doctor for a cough that wouldn't go away, we never even pictured how it would end. What if this is like that cough—something that seems normal but really isn't?

Move two spaces to see a doctor. Then get a call with results. Then—

"Are you sure I didn't hurt you?" Cat asks worriedly. She lets out a nervous laugh. "Maybe I don't know my strength. Maybe I'm She-Hulk."

I force a laugh. "I'm really okay."

I can't keep this up anymore. Every attempt to cover for myself only makes the lie bigger and harder to justify.

Cat speaks up. "Do you realize that, in just a few days, we could have evidence that UFOs exist and they have all along?" She collapses onto her bed, looking at the ceiling dreamily.

"Can't wait!" I say, trying to pretend that dread isn't creeping up in me alongside the twinge in my chest. Because, in that moment, I make a promise to myself:

After we find R.C. Fitzwilliam, I'll tell Cat I lied. I'll tell her everything.

CHAPTER
* 21 *

By the next day, the dull pain in my chest had morphed into something else. Did I really get injured from a *hug*? Or is this something else? I can't stop imagining my cells as little cartoons with hammers and chisels, making room in my chest for more garbage cancer cells.

I told Mom and Auddy I was hurting this morning, but they looked so concerned that I immediately under-played it. They were having a lovey-dovey morning, and I didn't want to bug them when it'd probably just work itself out.

The only problem? It's *not* working itself out. The acetaminophen I took early this morning has worn off and, every time I stand up from my desk, my breath catches and a tremor comes over me. Sometimes, I'll find a position that works. Then I'll move and the agony is like a deafening sound, overtaking every one of my senses.

After my first class, I sneak into the bathroom to take another dose. Cupping water in my hand, I swallow three gelcaps and move toward the paper towels. Starbursts light up my eyeline as my next step sends a sharp pang that radiates up my chest to my shoulders.

When I catch sight of my reflection in the bathroom mirror, I flinch. My pale skin betrays deep circles under my eyes and sweat gleams on my forehead. But the medicine worked this morning. It worked enough for me to fool Mom and Auddy, even. I just have to wait and it will get better. It *has* to.

I manage to make it back to class—barely—and drop into a desk. The teacher gives me a questioning look when she sees my face, but I wave a hand like nothing is wrong. Somehow, by lunchtime, the medicine works. I'm exhausted, but at least I can move. And thank all the lords of Nintendo for that, because today is our interview with Ms. Huynh, and Cat can't see me this way. Not *yet*, at least.

When Cat falls into step with me on the way to the library, I wipe my clammy, moist hands on my jeans and push them into my pockets. Even though I'm feeling better than a few hours ago, I worry that the pain is written on my face like an echo.

"Hey!" she greets me brightly. "Does Ms. Huynh know we're coming to interview her?"

"Yeah," I tell her, relieved when my voice sounds more or less normal. "I told her we'd come right after the bell."

Cat presses the tips of her finger together gleefully. "You know, we might make Regionals with this report."

I snort. "Yeah, and this project doesn't come with a mile-long list of codes to solve."

"Right? And who knows if R.C. Fitzwilliam even *has* something." Cat breaks off with a frown. "Oh, man. What if he doesn't have anything?"

I really don't want to think about that now, especially since my body will be dust by then if this keeps up. "Maybe we sweat the aliens out," I suggest half jokingly. "You know, go to San Francisco every night until we spot another UFO. With a charged cell phone ready to film."

"Oh, no. My parents would not be okay with that," Cat says with wide eyes.

I give her a sidelong look. "Don't you go out at night with Leslie and Zooey?"

"I always tell them that Leslie is taking us to her Korean bible study group. They're usually fine with any, um, bible activity. Should I tell them you're taking me to synagogue services?" She looks at me as if she's searching for a better way to phrase it.

"Hey, I don't know much better than you," I say with a shrug. "Shabbat? My mom raised me religion-free. We're humanists, or at least that's how Mom defines it. You could tell your parents I'm teaching you to make challah."

She holds the library door open. "Can it be shaped like a wreath? They love wreaths."

I arch an eyebrow, leading the way. "Suuuure."

Ms. Huynh puts up a hand for us to wait when we walk in, so I drop my backpack at the nearest table. Even though my pain has died down, the weight off my back and chest is a relief, and I let out a sigh.

"Are you okay?" Cat asks.

Oh man, she noticed that? Why do girls have to notice things when you don't want them to? "Um, I'm just tired. I'm carrying like five textbooks today."

Cat eyes my bag disbelievingly, and I don't blame her. It's not only a lie— it's an easily provable lie. Maybe I should tell her. Even if I don't spill about the cancer, I can admit I'm injured. It's not like that would require the *whole* truth.

Yes. I can do it. I'll just open my mouth and tell her, super casual . . .

"Sam! Cat!" Ms. Huynh breaks in to greet us. "Come on in to my office."

Or I could wait until after the interview. That makes more sense. And it will feel good to tell her something. Even if she thinks I'm a big old weakling for getting hurt by a hug.

"Thanks for talking to us, Ms. Huynh," Cat says.

"Of course. A few reporters talked with my family at the time and, as I told Sam, some students have asked me over the years. But I was young when it happened—only ten."

Cat nods somberly. "That must have been scary for you."

Ms. Huynh surprises us by laughing. "You know what? At first, I thought it was fun. My sister and I were getting ready for Halloween. My mother had finished our costumes and we were trying them on—we were these old cartoon characters, Jem and the Holograms."

I have no idea what that is, but I nod. A dull cramp throbs in my shoulder and I drop the pencil. Okay, the pain's not completely gone. Just stay chill, Sam.

Ms. Huynh folds her hands in her lap as she starts to speak. "The weather was strange that day. Hot and still. Heavy, almost. I guess they call it 'earthquake weather.'

We didn't have air-conditioning and the house was boiling, so we went outside. Linh and I were dancing outside, pretending we were pop stars. When the earthquake started, we thought it was a blast. We had no idea what was happening only two or three miles away." She breaks off, clearing her throat.

"So, it didn't feel that strong?" Cat asks.

"I didn't know how an earthquake would feel. Not a big one, at least. It was a roller coaster for two kids. And, since our neighborhood wasn't as damaged, we didn't understand how bad it was in areas by the water, or what happened on the bridge."

Cat looks a little green. "There was only one fatality on the bridge. Was it . . . ?"

Ms. Huynh shakes her head. "No. My aunt and uncle owned a local market in the Marina district. That area was hit hard. A fire started, and my cousin was trapped inside the building."

I almost expect Ms. Huynh to cry, but she says the words as if she rehearsed them. Like she's numb.

"That's terrible," Cat says, "I'm so sorry."

I know Cat is being nice. Still, something gnaws at me, and it isn't the chest pain. Cat isn't awkward, the way I was with Ms. Huynh last week. She says the words "That's terrible" and "I'm so sorry" with no real understanding.

She says it like someone who read about a tragedy, or saw it on the news. Like she's far away from it.

Dr. Wrongbrain tries to come in swinging.

If Cat finds out, that's how she'll look at you.

Oscar scoffs in response. *You don't believe this guy, do you?*

The smallest wave of triumph surges inside me as I realize it. I *don't* believe him this time. Because I know something he doesn't.

I can *trust* Cat.

After that horrible day last week, Cat told Leslie and Zooey about Oscar and both of them have been fine to me all week. Leslie even smiled at me a few times as if she were sympathetic. I don't know if Leslie filled Kevin in, but he hasn't stopped being a jerk, of course. I still catch him glaring, like I'm the one who did something to him. But Cat has been next to me the whole time, stink-eyeing *him* at every turn.

Ha! Oscar laughs. *Try again, Wrongbrain.*

Taking a deep breath, I redirect my attention to Ms. Huynh.

"Everything was swaying and warping for those fifteen seconds," she says. "Almost as if the whole world had bad reception. When the shaking stopped, we tried to go inside. But Dad ran out, telling us to stay outside.

We tried to call the rest of our family, but the phone lines were down. So, we sat there for hours—" She breaks off. "It's strange. That quake felt like nothing to us. It was over. But, in the Marina, the buildings were hit worse because the land is built on fill."

"Because of liquefaction," Cat says with a nod.

"Yes. Some of the buildings just . . . buckled under their own weight. And the power lines did too, which meant fires. The market—" Ms. Huynh breaks off. "A power line fell and the market caught fire. My aunt, uncle, and cousin Binh made it out, but Binh went back in after the shaking stopped. He wanted to get the money out of the register. That's when the ceiling fell in. After that, my uncle couldn't get back in and . . . it was too late by the time the emergency responders arrived. There was so much happening that we didn't know." Ms. Huynh shakes her head with an odd smile. "We were so close, but so far away."

So close, but so far away.

I swallow, hard, picturing Oscar lying in the hospital again.

"Thanks, you two. It really means a lot to me that Binh's story is told," Ms. Huynh says, but her words are starting to sound far away too.

Dr. Wrongbrain worms his way back in, and this time, he hits me where it hurts. An image of Cat flashes in my mind. And, this time, she's not acting awkward or distant like Kevin did. She's *crying*. And she's not alone. Mom and Auddy are with her, standing over me in a hospital bed. All the wires are disconnected, and the machine is off. Just like . . .

So close, but so far away.

You'll ruin her life too. Just like Mom and Auddy's.

My gut twists. *Shut up,* I think with all my might. *Shut UP.*

"I hope you have everything you need," Ms. Huynh says.

"Thank *you* for taking the time to tell us his story," Cat says.

"Yes, um, thank . . . you," I fumble. I still feel as though I'm trying to anchor myself back into the present, and it's not quite working.

Cat shoots me a concerned look before smiling back at Ms. Huynh. "Anyway, lunch period is almost over. We'll let you get back."

I move my mouth, and both Cat and Ms. Huynh are nodding. So, I'm sure I'm saying something very normal. But my mind is still flooded. No matter what happens,

Cat gets hurt. She'll be hurt that I lied but, even if she forgives me . . . will I hurt her all over again if I'm the one who leaves?

The last two periods are a blur of unwanted thoughts I can't keep at bay. Part of me wants to leave like I did last week, but my feet and head feel heavy again. And, to be honest, I'm not sure I could get out fast enough. When the bell rings at the end of History, Cat appears by my desk. She's still wearing a concerned look.

"So, are we meeting at the library today, or do you wanna go to my house, or . . . ?"

"Actually, I have to run home now," I tell her quickly. "Mom and Auddy wanted a special dinner-slash-family meeting tonight. Can we make a plan for tomorrow?"

"Um, sure," Cat says, surprised.

"Sorry," I say. "I forgot to tell you. But they were really set on a family meeting today, so . . ." I trail off, losing my own thread. Cat starts to open her mouth but I'm already lurching out of my desk and out of class with a wave. "Gotta run, but I'll text you later!"

"Okay," I hear Cat's voice behind me, small and questioning.

Mom and Auddy aren't expecting me home right away, so if I can get over to the drugstore and take another dose, I can wait it out until I feel better. Quickly,

I text Mom and Auddy that I'm hanging out with Cat.

Why lie? Oscar's voice rings in my head. *Why wouldn't you tell your moms that the pain is this bad?*

I will, I say in my head. Even silently, I feel like I sound desperate. *But maybe it will just go away. Right? It could just go away.*

I think you know better than that.

I squeeze my eyes shut. "Not now, Oscar. I just need to feel better enough that I don't scare them when I get home. I'll tell them, okay?"

He doesn't answer and, for once, I'm glad. I power through at CVS, taking another dose as soon as I'm out of the store. I have to dry swallow, and the bitterness of the pills dissolving in my mouth makes me wretch. Since I have time while I wait for the pills to kick in, I go across the street to Starbucks.

Braving the line, I get myself an iced caramel macchiato to completely block out the bitter taste. Then I sit and finish my drink, mindlessly playing a match-and-explode game while I wait. The pain isn't lifting fast enough, and I look at the clock on my phone desperately after taking one last slurp of the melted ice and coffee. It's been almost two hours since school got out. I *can't* be out any later or they'll worry.

"I know, Oscar," I say out loud even though he doesn't

pipe up. "I need to tell them. It isn't getting better." Even the words make my chest clench tighter, but I ignore Dr. Wrongbrain and the voice in my head that makes me afraid of what comes next.

I decide to buy Mom and Auddy's favorite drinks as a peace offering—just in case. A half-caf no-foam latte for Auddy, and this bizarre new candy corn Frappuccino that Mom is obsessed with. The walk is less than ten minutes but it feels like an hour.

As I approach my house, a muscle near my shoulder twitches and aches, and I try to rub the sore spot while holding the drinks. Twisting causes another sharp pain in my chest and I quickly reset my body.

"Mom! Auddy!" I call as I walk through the front door. Then I stop dead when I see them. All *three* of them.

Auddy looks panicked. Mom looks furious.

And then there's Cat, staring me down with a look of pure and total betrayal.

CHAPTER
* 22 *

The pain doesn't come back slow. It's fast, and loud, and all at once.

The sensation is something comparable to a giant claw, tightening around my body and threatening to squeeze until I don't have any air left.

"What are you doing here?" I ask, my voice coming out in a strange wheeze.

"Is that really what you're asking right now?" Mom seethes. "Where have you been?"

I fumble for the right thing to say but it only comes out as a bad excuse. "I wanted to bring you a treat. I got these for you." I hold out the cups weakly.

Auddy rushes over to give me a hug and I lean into it, afraid to tell her how much she's hurting me. "We're just glad you're okay, Sam. Cat came right after school because she was worried and, after what you told us about the chest pain this morning, we were *very* worried."

"I called your school, I called the Magnolia Center, I called the *emergency* room," Mom says, listing on her fingers, which she only does when she's really mad.

"Um, why? I'm . . . okay," I lie desperately.

Mom isn't here for it. "*Um*, because it's over *two hours* after school and we thought you would be with Cat." Mom gestures to Cat, and I dare to look over at her. She won't meet my eyes. "And apparently, you told Cat you were rushing home to meet us?"

"Sam, you had to know this would worry us," Auddy says, a hint of "don't mess with me" creeping in to replace her usual tone. "Why did you lie?"

Mom starts in again, but it becomes nothing more than a meaningless, muffled tone as I turn back to face Cat.

She knows, I think. They told her everything.

Everything everything.

"Cat," I croak.

"You lied." She says it so quietly I almost didn't hear her.

"Can, um. Can I t-talk to you?" I stumble over the words.

"You *lied*." She picks up her backpack and heads for the front door.

"Cat, wait!" I follow her outside and, thankfully, my moms don't follow me. "I'm really sorry, okay?"

She turns around, her eyes teary. "I don't get it. Why would you lie? Why would you tell me your friend died when *you're* the one who's sick?"

I suddenly feel like one of those memes where someone is surrounded by complex equations, clueless about how to keep the numbers straight. "Wait. I didn't lie about Oscar!" I exclaim, frustrated. What did Mom and Auddy tell her?

Cat lets out a thick scoff. "What?"

"I didn't lie about Oscar; I let you think it was *only* that. I have cancer *and* my best friend died of cancer. Two bad things can happen, Cat."

Wait.

Did I say I *have* cancer?

Dr. Wrongbrain quickly swoops in to answer.

You said "have" because it's back. It's back, and you're going to die like Oscar died.

"SHUT *UP!*" I yell at him, but Cat flinches in response.

"I'm so sorry, Sam. I would have understood if you only told—"

"*No,*" I cut her off.

"W-what?"

The claw grips tighter, so unbearable that I think I might need to sit down. I want to cry out, but I don't. Instead, I start to get angry for real.

"I couldn't tell you, Cat. Because you would *never* understand!" I shout the words, letting out a ragged breath and putting a hand to my chest. I can hear Mom's and Auddy's faint voices, but I don't care. "Instead of thinking I'm this horrible liar, or a loner boy, you would think of me as some wet, abandoned puppy. And then, if I—" I cut off, frozen.

If you die.

I shake my head. "And then you would just be *gone* because that's what people do when they don't get it. They bail, because they think tragedy is contagious or something." I suck in a long breath when I'm done, sliding down to sit on the porch. "You can go, you know. You don't have to stay here."

Why are my words coming out this way? It's not true. Not about Cat, at least. I know that. But I'm so tired.

"Sam." Auddy's voice becomes clearer as I finally make contact with the top stair of the porch and put a hand to my head. "Are you okay?"

"I'm *fine*."

Cat steps forward, but she suddenly looks like a watercolor painting—fuzzy and muted. I blink, trying to focus.

"I would never bail on you because you're sick, Sam."

I squint at her, struggling to keep the image straight, and then drop my head in frustration. "I know. I'm sorry, Cat. . . . I shouldn't have said that. I just—"

I look up and, suddenly, Cat is gone—swallowed up by these blurry shapes that aren't making sense anymore. I suck in air and my chest constricts, sending another wave of pain radiating up and down my body. Wait, where did she go? My mouth goes dry as I look around.

Did she . . . *leave?*

"Sam, your breathing," I hear Mom say. She doesn't sound mad anymore.

"Sam!" Auddy's voice starts to sound muffled again, and I don't see Cat anywhere.

Of course she left.

"Oscar?" I mumble. I can't even make out his shape anymore, let alone hear him speaking to me.

"Sam, sweetheart."

"He's *gone*. They're both gone." Crying makes the pain so much worse.

All I can hear is those words on repeat. Mom and Auddy flurry around me, putting something soft and warm over my shoulders.

I think I hear the word "hospital."

CHAPTER
* 23 *

I know that some amount of time must pass between Cat disappearing, being led out to the car, and Auddy driving through the long, circular driveway of the emergency room. But it all blurs together. Maybe it was fifteen minutes, maybe it was four hours. To me, it could be seconds between home and finding myself in a cold room, wearing a hospital gown and staring up at the PET scan machine above me.

"Hold your breath," the technician is telling me, even though the machine told me first. On CT and PET scan machines, there are these little emojis to let you know when you should hold your breath or release it. It's supposed to look like a little face smiling, then holding its breath. But it reminds me more of a smiley face that gets sick and barfs in its mouth.

I obey the barfing face when it lights up.

Then, like every other time, the lab technician looks at me with their best "p-p-poker face" and tells me in a dry voice that my doctor will be in to discuss the results. Of course, it won't be Dr. Krishnamoorthy, which bothers me. At least I've known Dr. Krishnamoorthy long enough to know her "bad news" face. This doctor might walk in smiling, and then tell me I have quintuple mecha-cancer and I can't do anything about it.

As the attendant rolls me back toward my room, I squeeze my eyes shut. Unable to get Oscar back, I try instead to picture a book. Then, I imagine myself turning the pages until it gets to the chapter that says "Sam didn't have quintuple mecha-cancer and he lived happily ever after." The image doesn't come.

"Hey, Cricket," Auddy says in a raspy voice when I get back to the room. "Mom is getting us some coffee." She furtively stuffs tissues into her pocket, her eyes pink, so I can tell she was crying before I got there. Also, she almost never calls me Cricket anymore. Guilt wears at me, even though I know it's not technically my fault. Well, it is a little.

I think of the time that Gemma Monroe is possessed by the spirit of this century-old murderer and almost kills Baskerville. It wasn't *her* really, but it was her body.

They conveniently ignored all the people she nearly killed at the end of the episode, but it makes me wonder. How my body can do all of this stuff without my permission. Am I possessed?

"How are you feeling?" Auddy asks me.

It's a simple enough question, but impossible to answer. Every single second, I'm terrified that they're going to tell me it came back, and the thoughts seem to multiply and repeat and crowd my mind until there's nothing else there.

Maybe my thoughts are a little like my stupid cells.

Still, I need to say something, because every moment of silence seems to deepen the creases around Auddy's mouth.

"The medicine is helping," I say finally, "but it's weird. I know the pain is there, but it's in Florida or something. Like it's far enough away that I don't need to worry about it."

Auddy says the right thing as always. "That's what it's supposed to do."

"I guess." I don't tell her the really messed up part— that every moment I'm in this place reminds me of Oscar. Every beep, or alarm (or, worse, long stretch of silence) is a knife to my chest. If I looked at myself in the mirror, I would see him. But the bad memories—not like the Oscar I've had with me these past few weeks.

If I ever did have him with me.

Mom comes back into the room after that, handing Auddy a steaming cup.

"How's the pain?" she asks me.

I sigh and jerk my thumb toward the other side of the room. "Five feet that way."

"Ah, pain meds." When she looks at me, her expression looks unsteady. Then, she quickly shakes it off like an actor getting ready to start a new scene. "Cat seems nice. I mean, when we talked to her. She didn't talk much after you *yelled* at her."

Mortification washes over me. *Cat*. "How much did you hear?" I ask.

Auddy looks at Mom, and then back to me. "We followed you outside, and y'all are loud, so . . . you know." She shrugs.

"Kiddo," Mom says, "why didn't she know? Why didn't you *tell* us she didn't know?"

It's at this moment that the pain medicine betrays me. Because everything is too far away from me now. Oscar, Cat . . . and every reason I had to keep this up to begin with. I'm too tired and weak and empty to lie this time. Besides, she's already gone anyway.

"Because nobody knows," I whisper. "Not really."

"What?" Auddy says. She looks at Mom again. "How is that possible? All of your teachers know, and the office. We picked up your homework for four and a half months."

The words keep spilling out and I'm almost *positive* I'm possessed by now. "On the first day I came back, I saw a note someone was passing around asking if I lied about having cancer."

Mom looks immediately irate. "Why wouldn't Kevin correct people? He knew you were sick. You told him after you started chemo, didn't you? Not that he was much of a friend afterward," she breaks off muttering.

"I-I . . . Cat told me he was the one who said it. Kevin."

Auddy's voice, usually as smooth and even as a blade of grass, turns to fire. "*What?*"

Tears streaming down my face, I keep going. "I don't know why he said it. Maybe he's a bigger jerk than I thought. He always acted like he was doing me this big favor hanging out with me last year. Or maybe he did think I was lying." My voice is thick and sore as I add, "I lie *all* the time now."

"What do you mean?" Auddy asks. Her body language

loosens a bit, and she exchanges a distressed look with Mom.

"I don't know," I moan. "When you ask me if I'm fine. When you ask if I'm sleeping, or if I still have a head-ache. Or if I cough, like, *ever*. This part of me knows I should tell you the truth, but then I remember when you asked about my cough after Christmas. I told the truth, and then it felt like one bad thing after another. If I say I'm fine . . . maybe I think I *will* be. Maybe all of the things that come after will just disappear."

"But you know it doesn't work like that, Cricket," Auddy says in her softest voice. "If we catch something early, there's a better chance everything will be okay."

"Yeah, I know, but . . . it still feels like it will ruin everything. All the fun we used to have all the time. It got so *hard* this year. And then, every time things felt like they were getting back to normal, some new pain would come up, or a test. Then there was Oscar, and that horrible week at the hospital. And don't get me started about the Crutchleys . . ."

Mom and Auddy blink at me as if this Crutchleys thing is coming out of nowhere, but they still nod along as I explain.

"That first day back at school, it got hard again. After school, I planned to tell you about the note. But then I saw the Crutchleys. I think it was the first time I actually saw one of them face-to-face in months. They said hi, but it was so weird. They kept tilting their head and whispering the word 'cancer' as if I just came back from prison. Like they were so worried about saying the wrong thing they couldn't get away from me fast enough. Then, I came in and you were making fried spaghetti and . . . I just couldn't say anything.

"Why?" Mom chokes out. "Why couldn't you say?"

"It would *ruin* it, don't you get it? It's not bad enough I got cancer, now I have to live this way, like . . . forever? Always worried that I'll have some ache or scare and that starts it all over again. And then sad about missing my friend, but also worried about how you would feel if . . . it *did* come back. If I was the one who was gone."

"Sam," Mom says. "I'm so sorry. I hope we didn't make you feel like telling us would be worse than keeping it inside."

"Or treat you differently than before," Auddy adds, lacing her soft fingers with mine. "We never want you to feel like you're on the outside."

"But I am," I say, my face hot. "I am on the outside. Because . . ."

"Because?" Mom repeats expectantly after I don't go

213

on. Her voice is so soft and weird. It somehow makes me even more upset.

The words bubble up inside and I can't keep them in anymore. "Because I'm not like *anyone*! I'm that kid in the neighborhood nobody wants to talk to because it's too tragic. At Chemo Kidz, I was the only one there with hair, and everyone else looked like the kids in the cancer commercials. Like I was some lucky kid rubbing it in their faces. And then there's school and *Kevin*. Nope. Don't fit in there."

I bury my face in my hands, feeling the hot tears slide through my fingers. The words almost hurt coming out, but I can't stop. "The only time I felt like I could relax this year was when I was with Oscar. He was sick, but it didn't matter. We played Mario Kart and Rocket League and *laughed* and it was the only time things made sense. But he's *really* gone now. For a while, I thought I had him back, but he's gone forever."

"Sam . . ." Auddy begins.

A delirious laugh escapes my throat. "I guess it's only you two now. So, congratulations! You have a son who's *nothing* like those commercials I keep seeing. You know, the ones where kids beat cancer and then become world-renowned oncologists, or gold medalists in mixed-doubles curling. Or even those inspirational kids in the cancer brochures who bravely laugh at clowns with their bald heads and no scarves. I'm none of those things. *Okay?*"

Once all the thoughts that have been flooding my brain are out, I stop crying. In fact, I stop everything except breathing. It feels weirdly calming to listen to my breath come out, slower with every exhale. We sit there like that for what feels like an hour, until I finally will myself to look them in the eyes again.

"Well, that's it," I say. "That's everything. So what do you think?"

Mom rests a hand on my shoulder and smiles. "That was all . . . really specific. I mean, why *doubles* curling? I guess I thought maybe javelin throw? Luge? You know, after you're gifted the miracle of a second chance of life, you really owe it to the universe to medal in luge."

Auddy always knows the perfect thing to say, but there are times that Mom just *nails* it.

It could have sounded insensitive to anyone else, but not to me. It was the best and funniest thing she could have said. All three of us break out laughing, and crying and then laughing again. It's so loud that it catches the attention of a passing nurse. When we settle, I breathe slower—looser. I had no idea how heavy this all was until it began to slip away.

"Hey, kiddo? What did you mean about having Oscar back?" Mom asks after we quiet back down.

"I've been hearing him," I murmur, turning onto my side. "At first, I was only trying to picture it, but then it felt like he was here. Like maybe he was protecting me. I mean, I'm not delusional. I know it wasn't him. It was only in my head. Only, for a minute, I thought . . . I don't know. It felt so nice to have him here that I didn't want to jinx it. Does that make any sense?"

"It makes perfect sense," Auddy says, reaching forward and combing her hand through my curls. "Everyone wishes they got to talk to someone after they're gone."

"But it wasn't him," I say. "Not really."

Mom says the words I never expect to hear. "Maybe it was, Sam."

I lean forward. "What?"

"I may not practice religion but I also know that there are things I don't know. When I lost Grandpa Bernie . . ." She trails off with a look I can't quite put my finger on. "Let's just say I'm a little jealous that you and Oscar had a strong enough connection that you could hear him. Whether it was in your head, or something we're not open-minded enough to understand."

The tears come rushing back so strong it feels like an undertow. "If we had such a great connection, why did he *leave*?" Then, I say it: my worst truth. "He just *left*. He left me all alone."

"Oh, Sam," Auddy says. She and Mom drape their arms around me, holding me as a few agonizing sobs rip their way through my chest.

"Maybe I'm mad at him for that," I say tentatively. "For being the only person other than you who I could ever trust with any of this stuff."

"Do you think that's why you yelled at Cat?" Auddy asks.

"No," I say. "I think I yelled at Cat because I didn't want to hurt her like . . ."

"Like?" Mom asks.

The words hurt coming out, so I say it in a whisper. "Like I might hurt you someday."

Both of them draw in a sharp breath. Tears stream down Auddy's face, making me feel even guiltier.

"I'll always be worried that someday the cancer will be back," I go on, "and that I'll make you feel as bad as I feel after Oscar left. Don't you see? I would be *doing* that to you. Just like I'd be doing it to Cat if we got closer. But it doesn't matter. She'll never talk to me again after today. . . ." I trail off, fiddling with the tape around my IV patch. It pulls on my skin until I feel a sting. "I guess that happens sometimes, though. People bail on you because it's too big."

Mom looks confused. "But Cat—"

"Oh, is this about what Kevin did?" Auddy asks, her eyes lighting up with understanding as she interrupts Mom. "Do you think Cat will stop talking to you because you're sick?"

I bite my lip. "Maybe that's why I didn't tell her at first. But lately it feels more like the reason I didn't want to tell you about the chest pain."

"Like it will pull you down a bad path?" Auddy suggests.

Nodding, I grumble, "It's not . . . *fair*. I already got cancer. I shouldn't have to worry all the time that cancer will ruin my whole life—not just my body. And other people's lives, too." I let out a humorless laugh. "Or that it will make other people turn totally evil out of nowhere."

. Mom stands, putting both arms on my shoulders. "Sam," she says. "I gotta tell you something about Kevin."

"Yes?" I swallow.

"That kid is the *literal* worst," she tells me. "Please don't judge other people by that kid. You're setting the bar *way* too low. As in, the bar is a tripping hazard, because that kid can, and I mean this, *eat my shorts*."

Auddy snickers. "And that's a Bart Simpson burn."

My eyes sting, but I laugh through it. "Yeah?"

Mom closes her eyes, as if the memory of Kevin is too much. "I hated every moment I was in that boy's presence. He was rude, surly—and, you know, he never said thank you when I made the best snacks of any mom in the neighborhood. But it wasn't only that. There was just nothing there. He was . . ." She pauses, searching for the right word.

"Basic?" Auddy suggests.

"Yes! *Basic.*"

They high-five, and my heart basically explodes with love for them. "I don't think Cat is like that," I say slowly. "But . . . what if she is?"

Auddy sets my phone down at my side. "Only one way to find out."

I stare at it like it might catch fire. "Maybe after we get home. I wish I had something more to say than sorry, you know?"

"What are you two sleuthing about, anyway?" Mom asks.

I open my mouth to answer, but a sudden *clack-clack* sounds as the privacy curtain is pulled back. A short Black man in a lab coat breezes in, staring down at a digital tablet. Which probably says I have quintuple mecha-cancer. Or that I'm spontaneously combusting.

"Sam Kepler Greyson?" he asks.

I almost don't want to tell him it's me. If I'm not Sam Kepler Greyson, there can't be any bad news. But then Mom and Auddy nod, the traitors.

The doctor looks at me with zero expression. "I have your results."

CHAPTER
* 24 *

Time slows down long enough for me to search his face for clues but, of course, I find none. Really? He's just going to come in and say "I have your results" and then nothing? He might as well be coming in to tell me that my Subway footlong is ready.

I hate this.

The vibe is so weird, and he's *still* not talking. Is he—

"Now, I know you were concerned with your history of cancer," he says in what feels like actual slow motion.

Spit it out, man!

"But I'm happy to tell you I see no evidence of that on your X-ray and PET scan. The diagnosis is costochondritis," he says.

"Oh!" Mom says with understanding. She and Auddy both seem to recognize the word, which sounds like made-up gibberish to me.

"It can happen after radiation or even sports injuries." Auddy pats my back. "It's nothing to worry about, Cricket."

"Absolutely," the doctor says breezily, apparently able to speak at a regular speed now. "Costochondritis is an inflammation of the chest wall. It's painful, and can feel very scary. But the condition should get better fast with the right treatment. It has nothing to do with Hodgkin's lymphoma, your mother is right. Occasionally, radiation of the lungs can cause inflammation that acts up for a while after your treatment ends. Painkillers without anti-inflammatories won't cut it. A regular course of prescription-strength ibuprofen and you'll feel better than you can imagine in the morning."

I barely hear a word of what he says after that.

It's not back.

It's not back!

Mom walks out with the doctor to talk about my discharge and medications, but Auddy stays, grasping my hand tight.

"It's gonna be okay," she whispers, kissing my forehead. "We're going to go home and watch whatever you want, and eat whatever you want."

She looks so relieved, and I feel it too. But there's

one tiny thought that stands in the way. How many times is this going to happen? I picture the old woman from the waiting room a few weeks ago—Lottie. She'd talked about this—the *after* part. Her words suddenly make complete sense to me. Is it going to be this way—with the scans, and worrying it's something worse? Am I going to have to hold my breath like that barfing PET scan light . . . forever?

Thinking about it makes me want to crawl in bed and sleep. "I want to go home," I tell Auddy, feeling like a little kid.

"Soon, honey."

Of course, in emergency-room time, "soon" means an hour and fifteen minutes, with another forty spent picking up medicine at the pharmacy. It drags, but it gives me time to fill Mom and Auddy in on all the *fun* things they've been missing—Cat and I solving codes, and our hunt for R.C. Fitzwilliam. By the time we're in the car and heading home, Mom is hooked.

"So, you two think that maybe that article got pulled for a reason?" Mom asks. "Like he has proof of a UFO visitation but the government won't let him say?"

Auddy, of course, is predictably skeptical. "Arielle. The government? Which 'government'? You're being nonsensical."

"I think we just want an opportunity to find out what he knows." I meet them in the middle as usual. "Maybe he did find some proof. I mean, he was a skeptic, like Gemma. But something must have happened to make him change his mind. For Gemma, it was when she finally saw the wreckage with alien technology."

"After a million years, when she could have been listening to James Baskerville," Mom says, rolling her eyes.

"Whatever, Baskerville-lover," I tease her. "Anyway, maybe R.C. Fitzwilliam saw something like that. Even if it's not evidence, I think I want to know what that *thing* was."

"The same Fitzwilliam who's been sending my son weird codes?" Auddy says.

Mom gives her a look.

"What!" Auddy throws her hands up in the air. "He's a full-grown man sending two cancer kids a bunch of puzzles. It's odd and a little shady. I said my piece."

Mom looks at me. "If you want, we can take you, you know. We'll drive you to the city and just knock on this R.C. guy's door. Even though San Francisco is a traffic-filled doomscape with nothing but left turns and hills."

"Really? You would do that?" I look hopefully at

Auddy for confirmation. She nods and hope blooms inside me as I clasp my phone again. If Mom and Auddy are willing to take us, and I solve the last bit of code . . . maybe I can make this right.

When we get inside, I find myself barely making it to the living room before collapsing onto the couch. I glance at the clock. Yikes. Nine thirty. No wonder I want to go to bed now.

"Do you want to watch *Otherworld*?" Mom asks from the kitchen.

"Do you even need to ask?" I call back.

Their laughter floats in from the kitchen, and I hear the familiar sounds of corn popping and their low, inscrutable voices. Auddy comes in first, handing me a small bowl of popcorn with parmesan cheese (my favorite). "Hey, Mom reminded me of something just now," she says.

I loll my head over to face her. "Yeah?"

"We got so off topic talking about that Kevin kid that we forgot to tell you something about your friend Cat. About how you said she bailed today."

I don't really want to think about that now, so I just shrug and make a little noise like "Whatever." Until Auddy speaks up again.

"You know, she didn't."

My head snaps up. "She didn't what?"

Auddy steals a handful of my popcorn. "Cat didn't bail. We walked you to the car, and then Mom went back to ask her if she needed a ride home. She asked if she could come with us."

I struggle to avoid coughing up my popcorn. "She did?"

"Yep. We said no, of course, and she told us she would walk home. But she was there when we drove away." She pats down the curls at the top of my head, but I feel them spring back up defiantly. "Thought you should know. I'm going to help Mom with the hot cocoa."

My mind races, trying to picture Cat staying with me. Nope, nothing. Maybe I got tunnel vision from the pain or something? Without thinking too hard, I grab my phone and text her.

Me: I'm back home/okay/not dead/not abducted by aliens.

Cat: . . .

Cat:

I watch the jumping dots disappear, and then the screen goes blank for long enough that my heart sinks.

Man, did I mess up. She tried to stay. And I just yelled at her when she didn't *bail* on me. I lied to her for weeks—even after she told me how good it felt to be herself. This is on me. I lean back against the couch cushions, defeated, when something sharp pokes me in the shoulder.

"What the *what?*" I mumble, turning around. A small stack of books is sitting on the side table, one of the corners poking out precariously. It's the code books Cat brought me. I turn and reach for the books, wrinkling my nose as a stench from my armpit hits me on the way. Blech. I guess that's what spending hours in the ER with no backup deodorant will do.

As I flip through the pages, one word catches my attention. I'm too far past it to go back, so I page through until I see what jogged my memory. "Come on, Sam," I mutter. "The painkillers can't be killing your brain *this* much."

Look at the shapes. You remember it from the code book; just FOCUS.

"Oscar?" I say aloud. After a moment of silence, I flush and look around, hoping that Mom and Auddy didn't hear.

It wasn't Oscar. I can see him in my mind, but it's not the same as before. His image is frozen, like a picture. Was it *me?* But I don't remember anything about shapes. The code looks like an alien language.

Frowning, I sketch it out on a piece of scrap paper. Getting nothing, I rip another piece of scrap paper and try to flip the code upside down and in reverse.

"Ugh!" I yell, letting the paper flutter down. "I give up."

But the way the paper falls makes something click in my brain. When I put the codes on top of each other, it doesn't just look like random lines and dots. It looks like . . .

"A box!" I shout, grabbing the code book to look for the one I remembered. "Xs and boxes, and . . . and letters."

I know I've seen something like it—these simple cross-hatch patterns, like sideways tic-tac-toe boards with dots and letters. "Yes!" I gasp when I find a page that reads "Pigpen cipher." When I look at the pattern, it looks similar to the one the overlapping pages form. But I still can't quite put my fingers on how to translate it into the code I see on the page.

Grunting, I pull out my phone and type in "pigpen cipher decoder."

When I get to the page, a smile breaks out over my face. There it is—each letter with a coded symbol that looks *exactly* like the cipher R.C. Fitzwilliam sent us yesterday.

I reach for a pen on the coffee table, but I can't find paper. Gripping the pen cap with my teeth, I rip it off and write on my hand, matching each symbol.

⊏⌐∧⊔¬⅃∨⊔¬> 23

FIVEPMSEPT 23

"Five p.m., September 23. This Saturday!"

I pump both fists in the air in triumph and chest pain shoots back up, hitting me deep behind my sternum.

But I don't care.

Not even a little bit.

CHAPTER
* 25 *

It takes every one of my Auddy-level lawyer skills to convince Mom to let me go back to school Friday.

"I'm sorry, you *want* to go to school?" Mom asks. "Who are you? Sam? Is that you?"

"I'm telling you, I'm fine," I insist. "Evidently, ibuprofen works, or whatever." I'm not lying about that part—since I started taking them after the ER, it's been way better. I don't feel perfect, but it could be a *lot* worse.

And I need to get back to school. Yesterday morning, I'd seen those three jumping dots, teasing me with Cat's possible response before finally falling flat, then disappearing altogether. Then, it happened again last night—twice. I thought about texting her a second time, but I'm not sure she wants that. All I need to do is get to Cat and show her what I found.

"I don't know," Mom says, tapping her chin.

I'm lucky I only have Mom to deal with. No way Auddy would have let me leave the house, but she had an early meeting and it's just me and Mom today.

"You can drive me," I say. "I'll go slow all day, and I *promise* I'll call you if I feel off. The ER doctor said it would feel better *basically overnight*. Didn't he? And it's been two nights." It takes a few more of these lines to convince her.

"All right. But I'm going to be working from the Starbucks down the street. Literally *minutes* away. Call me the minute you start feeling bad."

"*If* I feel bad. I'm telling you, I'm doing great."

Mom screws up her face. "Seriously, who are you?"

I shrug. "I'm Sam."

Mom's eyes glaze over with something that looks like pride. "Okay," she says in a determined voice. "Let's go. But I'm telling you. *Right* down the street."

After she drops me off at Northborough, I make my usual path toward the library before the bell rings. Cat and I met up there a lot before classes last week. As I open the doors, however, I see rows of empty seats. My heart sinks. Oh well. There's always lunch.

Somehow, I get through my morning classes, but it's a struggle. Every time someone passes by the window in the door of the classroom, I perk up, wondering if it might be Cat. I *have* to find her as soon as the lunch bell rings.

At the sound of the bell, I shoot out of my chair as though it's wired with dynamite. When I finally manage to get to the cafeteria at my self-imposed sloth speed, I see Cat, standing in line by the register.

Her long dark hair is pulled up into a tousled bun, like that day we met at the library on our day off. She's even changed her usual "Cat Pellegrini, model eighth grader" look in favor of leggings and an oversize sweater. She's not wearing *Otherworld* merch or anything, but something about her looks different.

And . . . I don't know.

Pretty.

She's too far away for me to talk to her, so I start toward her. I know she's probably still mad but she'll forgive me when I show her the finished code. I *have* to believe that.

Cat looks up when I get closer and I wave with both hands—a gesture I hope says *I did it!* But the moment she sees me, Cat's face moves rapidly from a relieved smile to a look of complete anguish.

Wait. Oh, no.

Is she *crying*?

Cat lowers her eyes, wiping her face with her sleeve.

Then, saying something to Leslie and Zooey, she rushes away from the line.

"Cat!" I call out. I struggle to make my way to her table, only to find a group of five guys wandering into my path. When I get around them, I blink. The table is empty now. Cat is nowhere to be found.

I exhale a ragged breath. She's gone. And she can't even *look* at me. Is it possible that Mom and Auddy were wrong about Cat? Suddenly I feel very, very stupid. Shaking my head, I drop my bag lunch in the nearest trash can and move for the doors. I'm so focused on getting out of there that I almost don't see Leslie and Zooey coming at me from the side.

It's your classic T-bone scenario. They cut me off at the pass, and I practically spin out, scrambling to avoid falling in the process.

"What's going on with Cat?" Leslie demands once I've righted myself.

"W-what?"

"She saw you and then bolted straight for the bathroom crying," Leslie accuses. "Seems like you did something."

I look nervously between them. "Um, it's kind of hard to explain."

Leslie's voice shakes. "Then tell us!" she demands.

"Because right about now I'm wondering if I was right the first time—that you pulled some prank about being sick and then made up another lie about your friend dying to get Cat to feel bad for you."

"Leslie," Zooey says in a warning tone.

"My grandma *died* from cancer," she says. "It's not something to joke about."

Oh. I blink at her.

It's at this moment that I realize a bunch of students are wandering over, quizzical looks on their faces. I open my mouth to respond, but Leslie doesn't give me the chance.

"Are you listening to me?" Leslie asks. She looks close to crying now, and I might be too at this point.

"Yes! I know it's not something to joke about!" My voice comes out so strange, I don't even recognize it. This is *not* how I wanted things to go. "I don't know why you assumed I lied about any of it."

Leslie's eyes flick over to her right, and I turn my head to see Kevin. Because, yeah, why not? I'm standing in the middle of the cafeteria, surrounded by what's quickly feeling like a mob. Why not throw Kevin into the mix?

As I glance at him, though, I see that he looks edgy,

like he's looking for a way to escape. "What?" Kevin asks Leslie, avoiding my eyes. "Why are you looking at me?"

Zooey fixes him with an incredulous look. "Because you were the one who said it. I was there. You told Leslie that Sam said he had cancer but that you were pretty sure it was all made up. Like it was some big joke to him."

My mind flashes back to the day I'd invited him over. I told him I had something to tell him, but then he looked so uncomfortable that I tried to keep it light. I may have even made a joke. Was this somehow . . . my fault?

But, hold on.

No.

Mom and Auddy gave him a lecture about wearing a KN95 that day because I was in chemo and Covid was still in its winter surge. They said it. *Chemo.* And I told him specifics—about my treatment, about how I'd be out of school. I only made jokes to make him feel better. I thought if he chilled out, we could get back to playing video games.

"Why would you think I was lying?" I ask him slowly, latching onto a specific point, "when my moms talked to you about wearing a mask around me because I was starting chemo?"

Leslie sucks in a breath. "W-what?" she sputters, shocked. "Kevin, you didn't say that."

Kevin scratches at his arm nervously, but seems to collect himself and turns to me with a glare. "I mean, it was weird. You ask me to come over and tell me you have, like, some terminal disease. And then you were joking. And you had hair. You have hair."

I stare at him for a long moment, unable to form words. *"What?"* is all I can manage.

Kevin doubles down, looking angrier. "And, you look fine, you know? What was I supposed to think? You look *fine* to me, bro."

It's a challenge, but I don't quite know how to respond to something so ridiculous. Did he not even bother to, like, *google* cancer after I told him? Nobody knows cancer can be deadly better than me, but it seems pretty easy to find out it's not terminal for a lot of people.

Several kids stare at me as if they're waiting for me to answer. Leslie's hand flies to her mouth as she looks between us, confused.

I close my eyes, thinking about what Ms. Huynh said about the minutes just before the Loma Prieta quake.

Earthquake weather. Hot, and still. *Heavy.*

The air feels that way right now, but the ground

somehow stays solid under my feet. I open my mouth, but I can't find my voice.

And then one firm, quiet voice cuts through the silence. "Stop."

I turn to find Cat stepping in, right beside me.

CHAPTER
* 26 *

"You lied," Cat says stonily, facing Kevin.

"No, I didn't!" he grunts, turning red. "I really thought he was lying."

Cat crosses her arms. "If you thought that, you're ignorant. Or just a really bad, shady friend. You didn't even ask him. You just went around spreading rumors. And, why—because he still had hair? What's *wrong* with you?"

Kevin looks like he might burst into fire, but he merely grunts out a noise in reply.

Cat rests a hand on my arm. "I know you didn't want to tell me. Or . . . anyone, whatever. But is it okay if I just say it?"

I nod slowly. "Yeah," I say in a thick, scratchy voice. "Go for it."

Cat turns back to Leslie and Zooey. "Sam *does* have cancer. Or, he did. He's in remission. His moms told me everything. And it sounds like they told him, too."

Cat points at Kevin, and Leslie immediately rounds on him. "So you did lie," she accuses.

Kevin actually looks like he might stomp his feet. "I didn't—he—"

"Get out," Cat says without blinking.

"What?" Kevin looks at Leslie and Zooey but Zooey lets out a wet scoff.

"Seriously, leave," Zooey adds, staring at him and gesturing toward the door.

Kevin looks like he wants to kick something, but he merely grabs his backpack and stalks off without a word. The group that had formed around us slowly parts to let him leave. After a moment, people start milling around again, leaving the four of us facing each other in a busy crowd.

"This is . . . a lot," Zooey says, her face the picture of confusion. "Cat, why didn't you tell us?"

"I didn't tell you because it's not my story," Cat says. "It's Sam's. And the last person we should have listened to is Kevin."

Leslie's face turns pink. "But, you were so upset back there. I thought he did something to you."

"I get it. But I was only upset because Sam *is* my friend," Cat says gently as tears spill from Leslie's eyes. "I care about him, and I thought he might be sick again."

I care about him. The words light me up from the inside and, this time, it doesn't hurt. I almost want to pull *her* in for a hug this time, but I'm worried it might crush me.

Zooey glances at me sadly. "I'm really sorry, Sam."

"Me too. I was a real jerk," Leslie says to me. She looks down guiltily and then back up at Cat. "Maybe I was a little jealous."

Cat blinks. "Jealous?"

She and Zooey trade a look, and then Leslie says, "It just seemed like you became friends so fast. And then, it's like you're here but . . ."

"But you're not," Zooey finishes when Leslie looks to her for help. "Like . . . we can't even tell if you want to be *around* us anymore. And we don't know what we did."

Cat looks sick. "I didn't mean to make you feel that way." She takes a shaky breath and speaks up. "Leslie, Zooey. I have to tell you something. I'm . . . a *nerd*. A huge, nerdy fangirl, actually."

Leslie can't hide a snort. "What? No you're not."

"Yes. I am. In fact, I'm a Trekkie. That's right. *Star*

Trek. Not Wars, *Trek*," Cat's voice evens out, turning giddy as the words spill out. "I believe in life on other planets. And . . . I still have stuffed animals. Like *thirty* stuffed animals. *And* I don't care about nail polish."

"B-but," Leslie fumbles. "You never acted like that was you."

Cat sighs. "I know. But maybe it's because you two are always so judgy about the kids who play Magic in the science wing, and about the Mathletes. And, remember after cheer that one day? You said Rose needed to grow up because she kept talking about the new Thor movie."

Leslie's face crumbles. "We never meant to make you feel that way, either."

I glance hesitantly between all three of the girls. Leslie and Zooey look shocked and I know what Cat must be worrying about—that they'll freeze her out now. But I'm not sure she's reading them right at *all*. They just look sad.

Cat glances around nervously when the silence stretches between us. "Oh man, everybody's looking," she says, reddening. "I've got to go."

"Cat, please wait," Zooey pleads.

Cat takes a meditative breath. "Look, I know this is my problem, not yours. You never asked me not to like all those things. I just . . . it's complicated and, right now, I *need* to talk to Sam to find out if he's really okay. Can we talk later?"

Both of them nod.

"Okay," Leslie says.

"We'll call you," Zooey adds hopefully, but Cat has already grabbed my arm and led me away from the crowd.

We walk out of the cafeteria together and then all the way down the hall, until the noise sounds only like faint buzzing.

"So," I say when Cat picks a spot, slumping down to sit against the wall. "I *am* okay, before we start. Just so you know. A doctor told me so and everything."

She lets out a reassured sigh, her arms dropping to their sides. "Really?"

"Yeah. Even better after that spectacular display in the cafeteria. You were . . . *awesome*."

"Yeah?" Cat asks.

"Kind of Gemma-like, even."

She flushes a deep red. "Don't say that unless you mean it."

"I wouldn't," I promise. "You might have a lot to explain to Leslie and Zooey later, but—"

"*If* they even call," Cat sighs. "They probably want

242

nothing to do with me now."

"They'll call," I say with confidence.

"I rambled on for like twelve nerdy minutes about my stuffed animals," Cat points out. "And I basically tossed Leslie's boyfriend out of the cafeteria." She facepalms.

"Um, did you see the way Leslie looked at Kevin?" I ask. "I think she would have tossed him out herself if you gave her a minute."

Cat looks back up. "Really?"

"Yeah," I tell her. "I think that guy's dumped. Also, Leslie and Zooey looked messed up about what happened back there. And you didn't exactly give them a chance to get to know the real you. Maybe give them a shot before you decide they hate you."

"Maybe. But, hey. Are you *sure* you're okay? You're not . . . um . . . ."

"No lies this time," I tell her. "Cross my heart. It's some weird condition I can't pronounce, but it has nothing to do with cancer."

She lets out a relieved breath. "I'm sorry I didn't text you back."

"Why didn't you?" I ask carefully, not sure if I really want the answer.

"Because I was embarrassed," Cat says in a near-whisper. She wipes a tear with her sleeve again. "After everything you told me, my problems felt so small."

A long silence stretches between us. It's exactly what I didn't want to hear—that I suddenly became this different person to her. The boy who wins at tragedy.

Finally, I say, "I swear, I'm still me. I don't want to be treated differently. *I* want to feel like myself too. You know?"

Cat looks horrified as she shakes her head vehemently. "No, Sam! I'm sorry. It's not that I couldn't be around you. I thought you wanted nothing to *do* with me. Then, I didn't text you back. It was mistake after mistake, and it felt like one too many to forgive." A huge tear slides down her cheek, and it almost looks like a magnifying glass moving over her freckles.

Relief washes over me. She thought I couldn't forgive *her*?

"I shouldn't have said all those things the other day. It wasn't that I thought you couldn't understand. Not really. I was just having so much fun with you," I tell her. "In my experience, cancer kind of puts an end to that. And, after Oscar . . . I don't know, it's really complicated. I'll just say this: I've lost a lot of people this year and I didn't want to lose you, too. I also didn't want *you* to lose me."

Cat's eyes get huge. "Sam, I would never do that to

you. I meant it when I said I think you're the best friend I've ever had. I might be worried from time to time but I hope you know I would *never* bail on you. I can't even imagine it."

"I know you wouldn't," I tell her. "I've known for a while. This is just . . . hard."

Cat smiles and pulls me in for a hug. I can tell she's being gentle because it doesn't even hurt this time. "Okay, then," she says. "Now that we've established that we're friends and neither of us is leaving, can we *talk* about that Kevin thing?"

I let out a laugh and it feels good. "Man, where do I even start?"

"It's so bizarre." Her eyes get wide and she shakes her head. "Do you think he just wanted attention?"

"I have no idea," I tell her genuinely. "I asked him to come over a few weeks after I found out because he'd been texting me about getting back into gaming. And I knew I had to tell him something, even though it's not like he was even asking *why* I was still out of school. He mostly seemed annoyed that I wasn't rounding out his Fortnite team."

"Ugh," she says, sticking out her tongue. "What did he say when you told him?"

I look away, frowning at my sneakers. "Pretty much

nothing. He got really weird, asked if that meant I couldn't be on his team. He looked so freaked I started to make jokes."

Cat gives me a funny look, but not a mean one. "What kinds of jokes?"

"Like about how I might get superpowers after radiation and be the star of the team. I said that I would have plenty of time to play since I probably wouldn't have to brush my hair for a while. You know, little stuff to let him know I wasn't different, only sick."

"What *was* that stuff about your hair, anyway?" Cat asks.

I give her a wry look. "Well. When you think of a kid with cancer, what do you see?"

"Okay. But to assume you're lying because you have hair? Really?" Cat shakes her head angrily.

"Most people don't know that not everyone loses their hair doing chemo. So, I don't know. Maybe Kevin thought I was lying because I had hair and didn't look 'sick.' Or maybe people really need to see a bald kid to believe it's a serious illness," I add, shrugging. "Like that's the cancer mascot or something."

"But why would anyone think you lied because you're . . . you know . . ."

"Not dead?" I ask.

"Yeah."

I pause, thinking about how to explain it. "Think about the books you've read with kids or parents who have cancer. Does that character usually live? Or do they die tragically, and the non-cancer character learns an important lesson about life?"

Her eyes widen. "*Ohhh.*"

"Mom and Auddy tried to get me a bunch of books like that after I was diagnosed. Kids with cancer. Most of them had that character die, but they had to make it . . . I don't know, *mean* something. I hated it, and it scared me. Sometimes, those stories even made me think I was going to die."

She looks down. "Ugh, Sam, that *sucks.*"

I shrug. "Those are the stories out there. Ones that don't really feel like *ours.* They get told by . . . you know, the lucky ones." I break off with a humorless laugh. "It's so weird, because that's also me. I got lucky *and* I didn't. But if I tried to tell Oscar's story, it wouldn't work. I can only tell mine."

"I think I know what you mean," Cat says. "You don't want to be someone's sad story. You're a person. You're Sam."

I beam at her. "I'm Sam. And maybe that's a little reason I didn't tell you. Pretending it was that simple felt good. When I hung out with you, I wasn't this kid with a dead friend who beat cancer. I was just . . . me."

"'Just me,'" she repeats. "I really, *really* understand."

Cat smiles faintly but then looks away, focusing absently on her hand as she picks at her thumbnail. Then she lifts her head to look right and left.

We're far enough from the cafeteria that only a few students are roaming the halls, but I wonder if she's checking for Leslie and Zooey. "I don't think anyone is listening," I say.

"It's just . . . I don't know if I ever told you what specifically happened after the UFO thing," Cat says in a low voice. "With my parents."

I shake my head.

"It was scary at the time, but then I was so excited afterward. I felt special, I guess. My parents didn't believe me, but I saw that coming. After that, though—" She breaks off with a heavy sigh. "When I got into *Otherworld* and the UFO thing, it felt right. Like I was becoming *me*. But they started calling doctors. They said my behavior was 'abnormal' and I needed to go on medication."

I flinch. "Wow. Abnormal?"

"Yes. They're never strict with Gia because she acts

248

the way they expect. They only ever get strict with me when I act like myself. So I learned, over time, that the only way I would ever get them to leave me alone was by . . ." Her voice sounds heavy as she searches for the word.

"Pretending?"

Cat nods, her expression pulled tight. I can tell there might be even more to the story, but Cat leaves it there. "Anyhow," she says, "I really know how you feel. I'm glad I got you as my California History Project partner."

I nudge her shoulder with mine. "Same."

Cat meets my eyes. "Although I am overcome with the desire to kick Kevin now. In the butt. Repeatedly. But at least we're talking again. I'm really glad to have you back."

Laughing, I say, "Silver lining?"

"Yeah." She sighs. "I just wish we could solve that last code. Part of me knows that finding out what R.C. Fitzwilliam wrote in that article won't prove anything to the world. Or to my parents. But what if it did?"

I press my mouth together, desperate to just blurt out everything I found in one long scream. I've got to play it a *little* bit cool, though. Like Baskerville. "Hey, Cat?"

"Yeah?"

"You'd better get out a pen and paper to take notes right now."

"Wait, what?" Cat laughs. "Why?"

"Because you're about to get *schooled* in the art of decoding."

Cat straightens, her face lighting up. "*No!* You didn't!"

"I did."

"You solved it?"

I reach for my backpack to take out my notebook. "Cat, my dear," I say, affecting my best Baskerville voice. "Get ready to go on an *adventure*."

CHAPTER
* 27 *

B y later that night, Cat and I had our plan to show up
for the meeting with R.C. Fitzwilliam.

It took a long phone conversation between Auddy
and Cat's parents, but they let her come to the city with
us. The best part was that there were no lies needed.
Auddy very calmly told them that we were visiting a
source that would help us get context for the California
History Project and that it could definitely result in giving us an edge in the competition.

This was, she explained to me, *technically* correct.
The best kind of correct, according to Auddy. She's such
a lawyer—I love it. She even listed other field trips she'd
chaperoned "to make them feel more comfortable."

When I woke up this morning, I thought for sure
I would spring up, ready to get that last piece of the

puzzle. But, for reasons I can't figure out, I find myself lying in bed and thinking about Big Things™ again. Not even in a sad way. It's just wild thinking about how much has changed since Cat and I got paired up on this project.

After I got diagnosed at the beginning of the year, I became this . . . offset version of myself. Sometimes, I even *see* it. Time moves strangely. People and places blur together and look like static. And my body has these stored facts that nobody else would need. Like, how to measure cancer stages in five-year survival rates, where all of my lymph nodes are, and what Reed-Sternberg cells are. It's not *useless* knowledge, but it still sets me apart from everyone else. Almost as if this Big Thing™ knocked me out of my dimension and I don't quite fit in.

Here's the hardest thing about not fitting: you still have to . . . be this *person* all day. You have to act like you fit even though you don't.

As I stare up at an alien head sticker on my bedpost, I realize something. Since Cat, I've started to feel . . . *tethered* to the real world instead of having to keep reaching for it. Like I'm in a tractor beam, floating in midair—but not in a scary way. I can finally stop fighting and stay in this middle place. Happier, and just . . . *me*—in between.

When I finally do pull the covers off and my feet touch the floor, I smile.

Sticking my hands into my curls, I glance in the mirror and puff them up until it looks like I've got a wild crown of hair. "Okay, Oscar," I say to myself. "Let's see what we found."

Saying my friend's name aloud makes me feel the tiniest stab of guilt. I haven't heard him in days. I shake off a fleeting thought that this new, in-between feeling might mean I'm even further from him. When R.C. Fitzwilliam tells us what he found, I'll know. And maybe I'll even hear him again. Even if it's just one more time.

After that, the day moves fast in a flurry of food, planning, and last-minute logistics. By the time we pick Cat up, it feels more like nighttime than four in the afternoon.

Mom twists around from the passenger seat as Cat buckles in. "You know, we might get there a bit early. Should we be bringing something? We could stop at the store and bring this guy some cheese or something. I don't want to be rude. And do you think we're dressed okay?" She waves a hand at her daily uniform of joggers and a T-shirt. "I mean, this is a conversation, *not* a heist, right? Because if it's a heist I should change."

I give her an impatient look. "No, and if you wanted

to ask fashion questions about the trip we're taking now, shouldn't you have asked hours ago?"

"It's just a supply check!"

"Of *heist* outfits and cheese. Mom. Seriously."

Mom brings up one limp hand and gives me a long, sarcastic round of applause. "Well. Played. Sam. You win this round."

"Arielle, I love you, but you *need* to leave those kids alone," Auddy says, tapping on the steering wheel. Then she breaks off and mutters under her breath, "Or else *I* might drive into an Arby's."

Cat giggles. "Your moms are funny. I didn't know moms could be funny."

"It occasionally pays off," I tell her as Mom pretends not to listen. "Let's go over our notes. When Fitzwilliam sees us, he'll know we lied about our age."

"That'll be obvious," Cat says. "But all we have to do is get through the door. He talked to Oscar, right?"

"We don't even know that for sure. That message he sent to R.C. Fitzwilliam was sent a few days before he got really sick. We know he got the scrambled response but we don't know if he lived long enough to solve it."

Saying it that way—as if Oscar is a historical figure or something—makes my throat catch.

Cat looks up at me. "You okay?"

"I'm okay," I insist. "I think Fitzwilliam will give us a chance. Even if we're only kids, we *did* solve his codes. That has to count for something."

She bites her lip. "Right. Okay."

The traffic is slow, but we eventually pull into a street parking spot a few blocks away from Vallejo Street. Soon, we come across a split-level house with a garage on the street and the address painted on the curbside: 28991 Vallejo Street. It's tall, and reminds me of the houses from pictures of Mom and Auddy's trip to Amsterdam. The rooftops rise steeply, casting long geometric shadows on the sidewalk.

I take a deep breath and look at Cat. "Are we going up?"

She nods, looking nervous.

Grinning, I wave a hand to lead the way. We walk up the long path, Mom and Auddy following behind, and ring the doorbell. After a moment, I hear a clatter, and then the door swings wide open.

A tall, bearded white man answers the door. He has thick eyebrows and deep divots on his face that remind me of potholes. R.C. Fitzwilliam looks between the four of us. "So," he says, looking away from my moms and right at us. "You two are the code-breakers."

Cat rushes to explain as if we've been accused of a crime. "I know I said I was a college student, Mr.

Fitzwilliam," she falters. "We're sorry."

He doesn't reply, but gestures toward Mom and Auddy with a nod. "You brought supervision? Excellent."

"We're only chaperoning," Mom says. "We won't get in the way."

"I thought maybe you wouldn't answer if you knew we were only kids," Cat goes on.

A hint of a smile washes over Fitzwilliam's face and he raises his hand in a gesture as if beckoning someone to the doorway. "First of all," he tells us, "never say the phrase 'only kids.' And second of all, I think we also have a confession to make."

"What is it?" Auddy asks with thinly veiled suspicion.

He clears his throat. "For one, I only found out about your arrival this morning."

"Wait, what?" I sputter. A muffled noise comes from behind the door, but whoever it is is still obscured.

"Come on, Row," Fitzwilliam urges softly. "They're here for you."

Cat and I exchange a bewildered look and then glance back to the door, where we see a boy emerge and smile at us sheepishly. He looks like he might be a year or so older than us, with golden-brown skin and a wild head of hair that puts even mine to shame.

"Um, hey," he says. "I should have told you before today. But *I'm* Rowan Fitzwilliam. I know you thought you were talking to Dad. But . . . I'm the one you've been talking to."

CHAPTER
* 28 *

It's all I can do not to let my jaw crash down under me.

What?!

I hear Mom hiss, "Ohhh, *twist*," under her breath, probably to Auddy.

Cat looks equally baffled. "But we called for R.C. Fitzwilliam and then you answered. I mean, we left a message."

"With Ed Lippi," the elder Fitzwilliam says. "Yes, I got that message from him, but I declined to respond as I haven't done an interview in years. What I didn't know is that you sent the same message through another site. And the only Fitzwilliam on *those* sites is my son. The other R.C. Fitzwilliam."

The boy shrugs sheepishly. "Rowan Chandrakiran Fitzwilliam," he says. "When you messaged me, you assumed I was my dad because we have the same initials."

"But why didn't you correct us?" I ask.

Rowan shrugs. "Why did *you* tell me you were *one* college student?"

I trade a look with Cat. He's got us there.

Another face appears at the door. It's a woman who looks a few years younger than R.C. Fitzwilliam, with deep brown skin and black hair pulled into a ponytail. She wears a sweatshirt that says "USF: *cura personalis*" and blue jeans.

"Hello. I'm Chhavi," she greets us easily. "Why don't we figure this out inside over tea. Maybe your moms would like to join me in the kitchen while the boys talk to you in the den?"

"Tea sounds great," Auddy says, beckoning Mom to follow. The three of them begin chatting, moving toward the kitchen and leaving Cat and me standing awkwardly by the door. Auddy glances back over her shoulder at me, though—a single look to say *We're here if you need us*.

Cat and I follow both Fitzwilliams down the hall into a cluttered den that looks exactly as I imagined it would. From the older Fitzwilliam, at least. There are floor-to-ceiling bookshelves and dark wood everywhere. The books aren't in a particular order, stacked horizontally in random spots. Without waiting for us, R.C. heads to his desk, riffling through some papers.

"Um, wanna sit?" Rowan offers in a quiet voice. He gestures toward a vintage-style two-seat sofa. I still can't tell if he's shy or completely humiliated by this turn of events. I'm still not sure how I feel.

I sit and motion for Cat to join me, which she does.

"So, you have the same initials," Cat speaks up, clearly trying to break the silence.

"Yes," Fitzwilliam Sr. says in a booming voice. "I'm Rowan Claude, but I go by Fitz." He slams down one folder and grabs another, flipping through furiously. "Now, where did I put it?"

"Put what?" I ask.

Fitz looks at us over his glasses. "You did come here looking for the piece I pulled from the *Skeptic*, right?"

My skin bristles with excitement. "Yes, we did."

"Well, while you and Rowan figure out your crossed wires, I thought I'd dig it up! Don't want Rowan to have put you through all that code work for nothing."

"Yeaaahhh," Rowan says in a long drawl. "I'm really sorry, you guys. You're not the first people to come looking for the article and mistake me for my dad. A bunch of Redditors have messaged us through the Foo Fighters and the Citizens of the First Kind sites."

"Us?" Fitz barks. "Ha! I'm not on any message boards."

Rowan looks embarrassed. "Okay, me." He stops and shoots a look at his dad. "But you were more than happy to let me do the forums."

"As long as you told me who you were talking to," Fitz grumbles. He peers at us again. "No offense. You two seem very nice."

"None taken," Cat says with an uncomfortable laugh.

"Anyway, when you messaged me, I thought your project sounded cool. Geophysics, right? I was curious, but I didn't think you'd want to talk to a lowly freshman."

"Same," Cat replies, sounding relieved. "Well, except we're in eighth grade. Sam and I thought we'd never hear back if it didn't sound official."

How is she being so chill? I feel like I'm outside of my body right now. It's at this moment that I realize I've barely spoken since we got here.

"But, what about the symbol?" I blurt out.

Rowan creases his brow, confused. "What symbol?"

I'd snapped a pic of the symbol weeks ago, so I take out my phone and hold up the screen. "This symbol."

"Oh," Rowan says, smiling. "That's mostly nothing. I wanted a sort of signature-meets-avatar for when I wrote on the message boards. So I made one." He shows us his phone, where there's a style board that displays the familiar icon in different colors and styles.

"So you did write the Foo Fighters newsletter last month," Cat says.

"I did," Rowan confirms. "And it used to be my profile picture."

"Used to be?" I ask, a sinking feeling.

"Yeah, I change it up every once in a while," Rowan says with a shrug.

It's all I can do not to facepalm. After all my obsessing over the symbol, it didn't even *mean* anything? Oscar had probably drawn it to lead me to the R.C. Fitzwilliam profile, but he died before Rowan changed his profile picture. I can't believe after all that, it was a false lead.

Rowan seems to sense my frustration, because he says, "But, hey, congrats on the codes! I'm really impressed."

Despite myself, I feel a rush of pride. "That last one took us ages," I confess.

"I mean, I kind of do it to weed people out. Usually people think I'm messing with them and give up." Rowan shrugs remorsefully. "Which is fair. I kind of am. But I'm glad you solved it. It's been . . . fun."

I can't tell if I'm annoyed or if I agree. Maybe both

are true. I open my mouth to reply when Fitz cuts in.

"Aha!" Fitz exclaims, holding up a single piece of paper. Which is weird. It seems short for an article that supposedly contains evidence of the existence of unidentified phenomenon. "Here it is. But, before I show you, I have to confess to a sense of curiosity. What led you to it? It was only up for a few days on the website before I asked my editor to remove it. It was 2013. Back then it was easier to remove things from search without a hundred people taking screenshots, but I'm sure there's a copy floating around in the internet archive."

Cat looks at me. "Just good research and cross-reference, sir."

Fitz removes his glasses and places the paper on his lap, agonizingly out of reach. "I see. And I'm sure in your research you've read about the ongoing Pentagon investigation and House Oversight hearings?"

My skin bristles with excitement. "We have."

"Sam and I read the whole transcript," Cat adds.

Fitz leans forward, cupping his chin with one hand. "Never has there been such an open discussion on extraterrestrial life and aerial phenomena. It's unprecedented. But there are still hundreds of reports that can't be explained."

"L-like the EQLs that were seen after the 1989 aftershocks?" Cat offers. "And the earthquakes in Haiti and Thailand?"

Mr. Fitzwilliam smiles. "That's a phenomenon I worked hard to disprove."

"I know," Cat tells him. "But, from the first few lines of your article, it seems like you might have changed your mind?"

Fitz holds up a hand. "Let me be clear. I concluded that EQLs are a terrestrial phenomenon—and I still believe that. It's most likely that they are a natural occurrence, similar to the aurora borealis. They're often seen after tectonic activity. There's an old Latin saying. '*Post hoc, ergo, propter hoc.*'" It means 'After, therefore, because of.' So many people assume that something that happens after an event must be as a result of it."

"Yeah," Cat says, sounding disappointed. "I guess that's true. Only it seems like such a strange coincidence."

I shift uncomfortably in my seat, sighing. Other than teaching us some Latin, I haven't heard any concrete answers. Part of me wants to reach out and grab the paper from his lap.

Footsteps sound from behind us, and I turn to see

Mom, Auddy, and Chhavi walk in and sit on the long sofa behind us. They're each sipping tea out of identical green mugs.

"I see you're giving them the *propter hoc* lecture," Chhavi says with a chuckle. "Don't let us stop you."

I turn back to Fitz. "I'm sorry, and I don't mean to be rude. Only—"

Fitz smiles. "Of course. Forgive the rambling. Here you go, but I have to warn you, it's a quick read."

Cat leans forward excitedly, taking the paper from his hands and setting it down between us. Right away, I notice it's barely half a page long. What the *what*?

For years, I had a mission: to prove that the "unexplained" wasn't so unexplainable. That was two weeks ago. Then, everything changed with one simple piece of evidence I could have never expected. The only evidence any of us really need.

Someone I love told me their story.

The account defied every bit of my current knowledge. It challenged at least a dozen things I know about science and statistics. If I'd wanted to, I could have plotted the whole story down to a sketch, asking a series of questions that would have surely cast enough doubt to refute the story. But, in a single moment, I had all that I needed— the moment that this person told me of a visit from an unidentifiable aerial craft.

She told me. And I believed her.

And so, after over a decade working for this paper, this must be my last piece. My armor of skepticism has been pierced by the only thing that truly matters: a human life. A human story. Ultimately, that might be the only proof we'll ever have.

For me, it's enough.

Cat speaks first. "*She?*"

Chhavi puts down her tea and smiles. "It was me."

"And me!" Rowan puts in.

"At four years old," Chhavi says. "And dead asleep."

"Whatever, I could have repressed memories," Rowan mutters. He, Chhavi, and Fitz share a smile.

Confusion bubbles up inside of me, threatening to

burst. There must be something concrete in her story. Right? Still, I manage to stay quiet and listen as Chhavi goes on.

"One night, I was taking Rowan with me to my office. I'm a professor at USF. Our campus has this tall hill that the students call Lone Mountain. I became accustomed to climbing those stairs every day." Chhavi breaks off with a laugh. "It was very late, almost nobody was out. I was carrying Rowan, when his favorite stuffed animal fell. I bent over and, when I stood, I saw it. Three lights, flipping on like spotlights and hovering over the tree line. I thought it must be a helicopter or a projection. But I had a feeling in my gut—it wasn't any of those things. Then, a single light drifted down—yellow and pulsing. I'd been hearing about military drones and the like, but this was different. One moment it was there in front of me and then, *boom*."

I flinch, my body still rattling with frustration.

"Did it make a noise?" Cat asks.

"No sound," Chhavi says. "It was odd because I could hear all the noises of the city before I saw the light. It almost seemed to suck all the sound *away*, actually. Then it burst into what seemed like a million tiny sparks. Each one floated back toward the three lights, and then it disappeared, one by one. As if it were never there at all. I could hear traffic again. Crickets, even. It took me five full minutes before I felt I could move again. I rushed right home and told Fitz, sure that a hundred other people must have seen it. But, nothing. It seems ludicrous saying it aloud now. I was standing on a hill in the middle of a city. How could I have been the only one? But I was. It made me doubt myself."

My head throbs. "I don't understand, though," I say, gesturing at Fitz. "If you believed Chhavi, why didn't you leave the article up? Why didn't you tell everyone that it was real? Why didn't you go to the news?"

"Because I asked him to," Chhavi says. "For me, or for Rowan. I asked Fitz to take the piece down, and he did. To be honest, I was . . . scared. For a year after I saw what I saw, I felt paranoid—as if this was all some kind of test to break me down. I worried that people would somehow find out what I saw and use it against me. Maybe I would get fired or . . ." She trails off and glances at Rowan. "Or they would take something more important from me."

"But, his article didn't name you, or go into any detail. And, even if someone did figure it out, you're a professor," Cat says to Chhavi. "I mean, you're *credible*."

Chhavi gives her a sad look. "The truth is, the minute you say you saw lights in the sky, you're no longer credible. What I saw was true, but the way the world perceives this phenomenon is also true. In some ways, that's the truth that mattered more."

"*No*," I say, shooting up from my chair. "Something is either true or it's not."

"Sam," Cat says. "It's okay."

I shake my head. "This is wrong. This is all wrong! Oscar said you had *answers*. He said 'We are not alone in the universe' like it was a fact. So, there must be facts."

Rowan makes a sudden noise and waves a hand. "Did you say Oscar? Wait, how—"

"Answers are *answers*," I cut him off. "Not more questions. I mean, how do we even know that's the real article? There's something you're not telling us and I want to know why."

"Sam," Auddy says softly, her eyes filled with worry. Mom moves toward me too, but I step back.

"There has to be a reason for all of this," I go on, my eyes welling up. "There has to be an *end*. Oscar needs answers. I can't go to him with *this*."

Mom, Auddy, and Cat all start toward me, but I spin around and run for the door, shutting it behind me with a loud *BANG*.

CHAPTER
✳ 29 ✳

Apparently, Cat drew the short straw.

"Hey," she says softly, sitting down next to me on the front stoop of the house. I look behind her, but no one else appears at the doorway. "I told them I wanted to talk to you first," she explains, seeing my expression.

"Ahh," I say flatly.

"Your moms are worried about you," she says. I make a noise, and she adds, "I'm worried about you too."

"I'm fi . . ." I laugh, catching myself. "Sorry. Old habits."

Cat doesn't avoid my eyes. "I know," she says. "And I know you're not fine, Sam. You told me a lot the other day about your diagnosis, but . . . we still haven't talked that much about Oscar. I mean, how you're *doing* after Oscar. Is there something you want to tell me?"

I take a deep breath. You can do this, Sam. You're not lying anymore, remember?

"After he died, I—" I break off, willing myself to go on. "Okay, look. I don't know how to explain this, but . . . it started to feel like I could hear him."

"He talked to you?" Cat asks gently.

"I'm not saying his ghost or anything," I rush to say. "Maybe it was all in my head. But it felt like he was still here."

"Maybe he was," she says without hesitation.

"I guess. But I thought if I could find out what he meant in that message that . . . Oh dear lord, this is going to sound stupid."

Cat scoots closer, putting her hand on my shoulder. An odd tingle spreads over the area where her hand is, and my throat goes dry. "Maybe I thought he would be here for real again," I say. "I know that's not possible. But if UFOs are real . . ."

"Maybe he could be real, too," Cat finishes.

I really want to cry right now, but something about Cat's hand on my shoulder is giving me this desperate feeling to hold it back. "I'll be okay. To be honest, I'm surprised you aren't more upset. I feel like I let you down too."

Cat smiles sadly. "I don't know. When Fitz and

Chhavi said all that stuff, it made sense. There has to be a reason why so many witnesses don't come forward. And why we don't have evidence even after so many sightings. And, here's the thing: *that's* what I was most afraid of. That, no matter what I say, nobody would believe me."

"Isn't that bad?" I ask.

"Maybe not," Cat says. "It almost feels like a relief. The worst thing I had on my list is true and . . . well, look at me. I'm still here."

"One less thing to worry about?" I tease her.

"You're joking but, yeah. It is. And if I don't have to worry about that, it's possible other things aren't as big as I thought. Like me, and the way I am at school. I was just starting to fit in for the first time in my life but . . . now I don't think I ever will. Maybe I'm not supposed to."

I snort. "Well, I may not be as chill as you are, but I know about *that* better than anyone."

"What do you mean?"

I blink, trying to think of how to explain my mid-tractor-beam feeling. "Before I got diagnosed, I never thought this could happen to a kid. This stuff isn't *supposed* to happen to us, you know? But it does sometimes. Bad things happen. I knew that after I got diagnosed.

But I was still surprised when we got the call that Oscar had died. I guess I thought there would be this cosmic scale—that the universe would realize this was way too much for one kid to handle. When I was wrong, I felt . . ."

"Angry?" Cat offers.

"No," I say. "I guess . . . jealous. Of everyone who doesn't know that bad things happen. And that there's nobody waiting to balance the scale, or keep the Big Things™ from happening again, over and over. Because cancer is a *monster* to me. And now I know what it looks like. Every time I feel something off, or I get a pain, I wonder if it's there waiting for me."

"Wow," Cat says. "That's . . . a lot, Sam. As in, that time Baskerville and Monroe found the alien mass grave with a million bones a *lot*."

"Never thought of it that way, but yeah."

"Sam? Can I say something?" She takes her hand off my shoulder and an unexpected wave of disappointment comes over me.

"Yeah," I say nervously.

"You didn't let Oscar down, either."

My breath catches. "How do you know?"

"Because you've been a good friend to him, trying to finish what he started," Cat says. She lowers her head, reddening. "Just like you've been a good friend to me. I mean, I don't think anyone else would have been psyched to help me prove the existence of unidentified aerial phenomena. Most people would say I'm loony."

"Hey, don't say that as if it's a bad thing," I say. "Loony people are our people. We see the world differently. That's *good*."

"That's true," she says.

"And, hey," I go on. "Maybe you could tell Leslie and Zooey. You never know. It could go better than you think."

"I don't know," Cat says, biting her lip nervously at the thought. "Even if they do stay friends with me, I doubt they'd believe me. I mean, I know you believe in UFOs, but do you really believe that I saw one? Even though you've never seen one yourself?"

I don't pause even for a second. Mustering up the courage of a thousand Baskervilles, I reach out to grab her hand. "Cat. I believe you."

She squeezes my hand and leans her head on my shoulder, her long brown hair spilling over it. Her hair smells amazing too—sort of sugary with a hint of raspberry. Is this the best moment of my whole life? It kind of feels like it.

Wait.

What *is* this?

"Thank you," she says as she raises her head.

Also, I like you, a voice in my brain screams. *I like you, I like you, I like you so much, please don't let go of my hand.*

It isn't Dr. Wrongbrain and it isn't Oscar. I think it's a new voice.

"You want to go back inside?" Somehow, I manage to pull it together and keep my voice moderately chill even though nerves are rattling through me.

"Yeah," she says. "Even if we don't have proof, I want to ask more about Chhavi's story. It'll be like we have this huge secret. And Rowan seems cool. Maybe there are more of us than we thought. Right?"

Laughing, I say, "As long as he doesn't make us solve more codes. I'm done with that forever, I think."

"Aw, but it was a little fun." She nudges me with her shoulder and I attempt to ignore the new screaming voice in my head as Cat throws back her head and laughs.

Suddenly, the door latches open behind us, and Mom is peering down through a crack. "Uh, Sam?"

I stand up. "Yeah, Cat talked me down and we'll come back inside. Sorry about how I acted back there. I was just—"

Mom puts up a hand, a strange expression on her face. "It's okay," she says. "Just . . . come back inside. Rowan has something I think you're going to want to see."

I glance at Cat, who shrugs and gives me a classic *Beats me!* face in return. We walk through the door together, and follow Mom back down the hallway to Fitz's office den. When we get there, Auddy, Fitz, and Chhavi are leaning over Rowan. He has his laptop open and points to something.

I clear my throat and everyone looks up with a start. "Sorry," I say. "We're, um, back."

Rowan gives me a funny smile. "So you're Sam."

This whole day is giving me whiplash. "Um, yes? We met, remember."

He shakes his head and stands up, laptop in hand. "Like I told you, I get a lot of messages from people thinking I'm my dad. I usually tell them they're wrong, or tire them out until they give up. Not a lot of people bother to get through my codes, but one other person did."

The hairs on my arm prickle as Rowan lifts the screen to face me. The dark screen shows a DM thread between the users baskoskervilleis1 and R0wanc@Fitzw1111am.

My voice comes out like sandpaper. "When?"

"Like a month or so ago?" Rowan says. He peers at

the screen. "Yeah, look. I got his response on August second. Just read a bit, okay?"

I obey, dragging my eyes back to the screen even though I'm almost feeling afraid to.

Baskoskervilleis1: anne reeta wool = we are not alone. Amirite?

Baskoskervilleis1: And if I *am* right, can I ask you a few questions? My name is Oscar Padilla and I'm looking for an article by an R.C. Fitzwilliam. Is that you by any chance?

R0wanc@Fitzw1111am: Lt srlegn1oaino oa cis ihig 91coflepsts9

Baskoskervilleis1: Ahhhh, a wise guy, huh? All right, all right.

Baskoskervilleis1: Ha! Joke's on you, I'm in bed all day and I've got nothing but time. I see you're a fan of the rail fence cipher. I'm a fan now too! So, "Lt srlegn1oaino oa cis ihig 91coflepsts9" translates to "Location of solar eclipse sightings 1991," and my answer would be MEXICO CITY. Ding ding! I think next I'll take 20th century PC games for 800.

I laugh out loud as I read that last one, putting a hand to my face. "Oscar loved *Jeopardy!*," I explain.

R0wanc@Fitzw1111am: Ok, ok, you win. I'm impressed. But I don't think I can help you with the article. I'm not who you think I am.
Baskoskervilleis1: That's okay. But you obviously know something about UFOs.
R0wanc@Fitzw1111am: I know what I research

I keep skimming, but so much after that is just conversation.

"I'll send you the whole thing," Rowan says. "Sorry it's so long. We messaged for like five hours. But, there was one thing I thought you might want to read—at the end here." He takes the laptop, dragging his finger down the mouse pad for a few seconds, and then hands it back to me.

Baskoskervilleis1: Hey, so I don't know if this is weird, but my friend and I have been in research mode for months about this. Wanna join forces??

R0wanc@Fitzw1111am: I'm not really a . . . joiner

Baskoskervilleis1: That's okay, neither are we. And I can vouch for Sam, you know. He's in it for proof.

R0wanc@Fitzw1111am: You're not?

Baskoskervilleis1: I just like looking at the stars. But I wouldn't mind if I saw something else one of these days. Look, just set up a chat for us. I swear, Sam's good people. He's my best friend, and I don't say that lightly. Honestly, he's one of the funniest, craziest, all-around BEST people in the world. A true sign that intelligent life exists on our planet. If you trust me, you trust him.

R0wanc@Fitzw1111am: Why does it feel like you're setting me up on a date with your friend?

Baskoskervilleis1: Please! I don't think I could set that boy up on a date with anyone but Gemma Monroe. We could just use the proof that there are more like us. And I want to give him something. He gave me this whole summer. I swear, no joiner energy. Just a good old-fashioned chat between lone wolves.

R0wanc@Fitzw1111am: Ok, get me his screen name and I'll set up a chat.

Baskoskervilleis1: He's not on this site yet. I'll talk to him later and get back to you. Stay tuned!

I can't hold back the tears long when I realize the chat ends there. The next morning, Oscar was taken to the hospital, and two weeks later, he died.

For a full minute, I sit in stunned silence. Then Cat reaches over and rests a hand on my arm. The tingle comes back, and I feel warm all over like she covered me with a big blanket.

"Thanks," I say to Rowan, wiping my cheek. "He . . . got really sick right after this."

"I told them," Auddy says, wrapping her arms around me.

All of us are so quiet, and I feel like I need to be the one to break the silence. But a million questions are racing around in my head. Did Oscar try to call me that day? Did he know he was getting sicker? Then Cat asks the question that rings loudest:

"Do you think he knew?"

Did Oscar know what—that he was about to get so sick he couldn't come back from it? I focus all my effort and ask him myself.

Were you trying to make sure I wouldn't be alone? I ask him.

Then, in one incredible moment, I can hear him again. Oscar, deep and embedded inside my mind . . . laughing his butt off.

Color you self-involved, Oscar says through giggles. *Like I'm going to spend my final days setting you up on some nerd man-date? Sorry, buddy.*

I can't help it. I laugh too.

"Sam?" Mom murmurs.

"It's okay," I say. "For real this time. And to answer your question, no. I don't think he knew. But it doesn't matter. It's just nice seeing him call me his best friend again."

"I'll send you the whole thing," Rowan says again, his eyes downcast. "I'm . . . really sorry about your friend."

Fighting the urge to respond with my usual 'It's okay," I say, "Thanks. It pretty much sucks."

"Well said," Fitz says.

"I wish I'd had more time to get to know him," Rowan says, setting his laptop back down and taking a seat. "I mean, we only chatted for a day, but he felt like someone I'd be friends with. I wish I knew more."

"He was awesome."

"Why don't you tell us about him?" Chhavi suggests in a soft voice.

"Yeah?" I ask.

"I want to hear more too," Cat says.

Auddy squeezes my shoulders. Then, Mom kneels next to my chair and grabs my hand. I inhale a long, deep breath.

Then I tell them all about the brave and fearless Oscar Padilla.

CHAPTER
* 30 *

"When we see pictures of a natural disaster, it's easy to focus on the physical damage," Cat's voice rings out. "It's also easy to forget the long-term toll it can take on people."

I glance down at my note card as I read on. "The Loma Prieta earthquake caused six billion dollars in damage, and nearly another two billion to reinforce structures and make them more earthquake-safe. That'd be the equivalent of almost thirty billion today. But money wasn't the only thing lost. Sixty-three people died in the quake." Raising my eyes, I see hundreds of faces looking back at me.

"But more than just those sixty-three were impacted," Cat follows. "The lives of their families and friends would be changed forever. And that can never be paid back, or replaced. California lawmakers have fought to change building codes, and make our trains and roadways more earthquake-safe. Years of retrofitting means that we're more ready for the next big one than they were. But reconstruction isn't only about the homes, roads, and bridges." She glances at me. "It's about helping people to move on from a trauma they should have never had to endure."

My voice shakes a bit as I speak up next, because I can't help thinking about Oscar and Chhavi, and how much one life can shape everything.

"In doing our project," I continue, "we wanted to recognize the impression those lives left on us. So, please keep the handout we gave you at the beginning of the presentation. It lists every person, and many beloved pets, who were lost that day. Because walls can be rebuilt, but lives can't. In doing this, and naming those people, we hope that you remember those who perished, but also that you remember not to take those in your life for granted."

Then, Cat and I take turns naming the people who died in the earthquake. I catch Ms. Huynh's eye when we say Binh's name, and she smiles. After we're done and take our bow, a round of applause sounds, and Cat and I grin at each other triumphantly.

"Not bad," I whisper to Cat as we head toward our seats.

"Same," she whispers back.

On our way to the back row, I glimpse Kevin out of the corner of my eye. He's stubbornly looking away from me, his arms folded as he stares off to the opposite side of the auditorium. Cat must see him too, because she rolls her eyes.

"What a baby," she says. "Maybe when he does his presentation, we should hand him a bouquet of diapers."

I choke on a snort. "You're a good friend."

She gives me a somewhat evil smile in reply and we share a secret laugh.

Cat and I take our seats and watch the rest of the presentations. I might be biased, but I still think Cat and I knocked it out of the park with ours. Although I was impressed that Leslie and Wei turned the tables on their colonialism report, talking about each tribe that had land stolen from them. They even had quotations from the director of Native and Indigenous Studies at UC Berkeley. So, we might not make Regionals, but I'm fine with that.

"Oh, look! My parents are here," Cat says, beaming.

After our road trip, Cat sat her parents down to have a serious "Talk with a capital T," as she called it.

"How was yesterday?" I ask her in a low voice.

"Not . . . terrible," Cat says. "It's a start, at least. I didn't bring up my sighting. I don't think my parents will ever believe that. But I did tell them how they've been making me feel. They still acted like studying paranormal stuff is a gateway to witchcraft, and I almost bailed. But then Gia told them they were being ridiculous. I think they might have actually listened. Who knows?" Cat laughs and gives me a wave. "I'll find you after I talk to them, okay?"

I scan the crowd, looking for Mom and Auddy. I know both of them took the day off to come to the presentation. The crowd is so thick, I can barely place one person from another, so I duck outside to the courtyard, where the crowd is thinner and I can actually hear myself think. I veer toward a bench on the side of the breezeway when two familiar faces step into view.

"Hey, Sam," Leslie greets me, wringing her hands. Zooey waves from behind her.

I look around for any excuse to bail, but come up short. "Hey."

"So . . . we talked to Cat this weekend," Leslie says. "But she's still acting weird."

I raise an eyebrow. "Weird?"

"No, I mean—um—" Leslie's eyes dart around, as

if looking for someone to rescue her. When she doesn't find anyone, she moans, burying her face in her hands.

"She sounded like she did last month," Zooey clarifies. "Like nothing happened."

I shrug. "Okay. How is that different from the situation you had before?"

"Because now we know!" Leslie blurts, turning bright red. "That she's acting around us. That she likes all these things we don't even know about. I mean, who cares if she likes science fiction? I don't, but whatever!"

Putting on my best therapist voice, I ask, "Did you tell *her* that?"

Leslie and Zooey trade a miserable look. "No," says Zooey.

I let out a long sigh. "Look, I know she still wants to be friends. Why don't you just . . . ask her about herself?"

Leslie looks up, her eyes brightening. "You mean, like we're only meeting her now?"

"That works. Maybe ask about her favorite shows or something."

"Okay!" Leslie says. "Can you tell her we want to talk?"

"Oh, and can you tell her I believe in unicorns?" Zooey adds.

"What?" Leslie and I say in unison.

Zooey shrugs. "What? Is it so unbelievable that at one time, horses had horns? Evolution, y'alls."

"Okay," I say, giving them a funny look. "I'll tell Cat that you want to talk . . . and that you believe in unicorns."

"Thank you!" Zooey says, pressing her hands together.

"Oh, and Sam?" Leslie says as I'm turning away.

"Yeah?"

"I shouldn't have believed Kevin. Only . . . I thought you were making *fun* of cancer or something. After my grandma—"

"I get it," I say. And I do. Because Leslie had her own Big Thing™—something I didn't even know about. And maybe it made her be kind of a troll to me, but I can see why.

"Still, it was wrong," Leslie insists. "And I'm sorry."

"I'm sorry too, Sam," Zooey tells me. "I will never believe anything that boy says again."

Leslie tosses her eyes up. "Kevin's been asking me to hang out for a while. I almost wonder if he made it up just so he could get attention long enough for me to talk to him."

"I . . . wouldn't put it past him," I say with great restraint.

"Well, I'm not speaking to him anymore," Leslie says.

"And his presentation was barely D-level so, you know, karma."

I can't hide a snort of laughter. "Yeah. Karma."

Leslie smiles. "Great job today. You and Cat *almost* came close to beating me and Wei."

"We'll see," I say ominously.

"*We'll* see," Leslie counters.

"Yeah, well, you know what we're gonna have to do? *See.*" I fold my arms over my chest, smirking.

Leslie points two fingers at me. "I got my eyes on you, Kepler Greyson. And my ears. And my . . . nose."

"I guess I should try to shower more regularly, then."

Zooey laughs and Leslie gives me a slow clap. "Not bad. See you around, Sam."

"See you."

Before I can marvel at how weird it feels to be *smiling* after a conversation with Leslie and Zooey, I hear a familiar voice.

"Cricket!" Mom calls, breaking through the buzz of the crowd. She's leading Auddy and Cat along with her. Then, she puts a hand over her mouth. Then she whispers, "I mean, Sam."

I try not to facepalm. "You said the wrong part loud, Mom," I tell her when she gets close enough. Cat giggles and I can feel my cheeks turn beet-red.

"We're so proud of you two!" Auddy says, resting a hand on both our backs. "Arielle thought we'd treat you both to dinner."

I give Cat a searching look. "Aren't your parents taking you out?"

"Gia is out tonight, so we made a plan to celebrate Wednesday instead," Cat says. "I asked them if it was okay, and they said yes." She beams, clearly excited not to have to create an elaborate ruse just to hang out with me.

"We were thinking of La Victoria," Mom adds, and I immediately start drooling.

"Ohhh. I do love La Vic," Cat says. "That special sauce is everything."

"Agree," I say with a serious nod. "I made Mom and Auddy take me there after almost every one of my infusions. Cancer perks!"

"Cancer peeerrrks," Mom repeats in a funny a capella-style singsong voice.

Cat's eyes pop, and she makes a sputtering sound. "Um, what?"

Mom, Auddy, and I all trade a laugh.

"There's not many upsides to having cancer," I tell her. "In fact, it's uhhh . . . the *worst*. So, when you get something special because you have cancer . . ."

"Free valet service at the hospital!" Auddy puts in.

"Getting out of a speeding ticket," Mom adds.

"Wait, what was that one?" I ask her.

Mom puts on an exaggerated pouty-face. "I'm sorry I was speeding, Officer. I'm picking up my son from *radiation* treatment." She lets out a theatrical sob and Auddy and I snort with laughter.

"Anyhow, you take the wins where you can," I say.

Cat still looks mildly horrified, but she manages a laugh. "Okay. If a great burrito is a cancer perk . . . I guess I'm happy to be along for the ride?"

"Well, then, it's settled!" Mom says, clapping her hands together.

Once we make our way out to the parking lot, we all pile into Auddy's car and head toward the hills. It's not quite dusk, but the sky already looks dimmer over the trees.

"Why does the hill say 'South San Francisco: The Industrial City' again?" I ask nobody in particular, as we get closer and the words appear in my eyeline.

"I don't know. Was it because of the World Fair, maybe?" Mom says. "I'll google it." A minute later, she looks at us, downtrodden. "I read every word of that Wikipedia article but I still don't understand."

"Maybe it's supposed to be like 'The City of Progress'?" Auddy suggests.

"Then why wouldn't they *say* that?" I point out.

Auddy rolls her eyes in reply. "So many questions."

"It's better than 'The City of Strip Malls,'" Cat says with a laugh.

"Or 'South San Francisco: *You're Almost to the Airport,*'" Mom adds.

"How about 'City of the Dead'?" I ask.

"Nah, that's Colma," Auddy tells me. "At least we have *some* living people."

"Huh. I guess that really is the best thing we can come up with," Cat says. "'The Industrial City.' So weird."

"Speaking of weird," I whisper in Cat's ear. "You know what we're close to?" I point at the sign for Don Francisco Cemetery, where Cat had her close encounter.

"I know," she hisses. "Look, we can just forget about it. Nobody's ever going to believe me other than you. I might as well have made it up."

"What? Come on, you don't mean that."

She crosses her arms and sighs. "No. I don't. But it still feels weird talking about it. Even though I know what I saw."

I fall silent for a moment, but then turn back to her.

"Hey, you know Theodore Roosevelt?"

She snorts. "You mean, personally?"

"Duh, no."

"Then why are you asking? Why wouldn't I know who Theodore Roosevelt is? Do you think I've never read a book?"

"Ahhh!" I moan with frustration. "Sorry, I was only trying to bring him up. Anyway, he has this famous quotation that they used in the opening credits to an episode of *Otherworld*."

"Which one?"

"The one where Baskerville finds out that his contact has been lying to him, and he starts doubting everything. Remember, he gets depressed and eats five pies?"

"Oh yeah! Such a good one."

"Yes! Anyway, he has this famous quotation, 'Keep your eyes on the stars, and your feet on the ground.' It's supposed to mean that you should be realistic but also believe in yourself or something. But I think it has another meaning. Stay focused, but never lose your belief in something bigger than you can see right now. It's exactly like the stars. To us, they're these little light dots in the sky. But, to someone on another planet, they might look like the sun. We only *know* the things we can prove. But that doesn't mean the other stuff isn't true."

"Yeah," she says. "Eyes on the stars. I *love* that."

"Good," I say, peering out the window. Auddy pulls into the parking lot of La Victoria, and I glance up toward the sun lowering behind the hill. "Because I have a plan."

CHAPTER
∗ 31 ∗

An hour later Cat and I have burritos in hand, and we're sitting on the lawn at Don Francisco Cemetery. Mom and Auddy agreed to let us walk up as long as I turned on my phone tracker—so they'd know where we were at all times.

"This is ridiculous!" Cat laughs. "We're not going to see anything."

"Hey, how do you know?" I ask. "Maybe this particular UFO loves to come look at the beautiful view." I sweep my hand dramatically at the very boring hill in front of us.

Cat busts up laughing, and unwraps her burrito. "You have been weirdly funny today."

"Weirdly funny?"

"Yeah."

"I guess I feel good because . . . I'm glad we became friends." I lie down on the lawn, gazing up at the now-darkened sky. "Hey, speaking of which: I got the full details from Rowan. Silicon Valley Comic Con tickets are ours."

"Yes!" Cat says, pumping her fist. "Did you hear they might be dropping a new *Otherworld* graphic novel from Dark Horse? Maybe even in time for the convention."

"That wouldn't suck," I say with a laugh. "Your parents are cool with us going?"

She sighs, reclining next to me. "I hope so. Keep your fingers crossed."

"Hey, if they say no, maybe you can tell them the comic con is sponsored by Leslie's Korean bible study group. Eh? Ehhhh?"

Cat cackles. "See? Weirdly funny. You have to admit it."

I look at her thoughtfully. "Yeah. I think maybe that was Oscar's doing. Hearing him that way—in his voice reminded me that I am funny. That *funny* and *sad* can happen all at once."

"I like that," she says, turning to face me. "Hey— you know, all this earthquake research made me realize something."

I prop myself up on one elbow and nod for her to go on.

"You know how we learned about the San Andreas fault, and how it builds up over time, and then one side can sort of slip under the other?"

"Yeah."

"I think *I* feel that way sometimes," Cat says, facing toward the sky again. "After I said the name 'Cat' at the beginning of the year, I had to hold everything in place. The pressure was too much. Every day, I came home and I thought: there's another day I made it through. But then I would get afraid. What if I couldn't make it through the next day. Or the next one?"

"But you are," I point out softly. "Making it through. Right?"

"So are you," she says, tilting her head to look at me.

I feel way too nervous to meet her gaze. "Yeah?"

"Yeah. And I hope you think I am. I mean . . . you can tell me when you miss Oscar. Or when you're freaking out about resu . . . recoun . . . wait, what's that word again?"

"A recurrence," I say, stealing a glance. "But it's just a fancy word for the cancer coming back. I think I'll always be freaking out about that."

A dull pit forms in my gut, and it's not me being sad, or Wrongbrain coming back. It's this new part of my mind that can't stop thinking about how close Cat's arm is to mine.

"I wish you didn't have to be scared forever," Cat says.

"Me too."

"Yeah." She sighs.

"But, if you're asking, you are a good friend. You . . . broke me out of something."

She turns to face me again and, this time, I manage to meet her eyes. "What does that mean?" she asks.

"After Oscar died, I kept pushing and pushing, trying to force myself to be okay. The day you came over to my house and found out—that was necessary. I told my moms, like, *everything* that's been going on with me. It needed to happen, and you helped me get there. Even if what you did was . . . get yelled at." I break off remorsefully. "Sorry again."

Cat crosses her arms behind her neck and stares at the sky again. "That's okay. We helped each other, right?"

I turn my face just enough to see her in profile. "Right."

"Which makes us pretty lucky." She sighs and then turns her hazel eyes on me, taking one hand from behind her neck and letting it fall down beside me.

This is the moment! my brain screams. *If you want to hold her hand, it's now. Now!*

Even thinking this totally freaks me out, of course, so I go the opposite route and put both my hands behind my head. To make it look like I'm not in a full panic, I do what I do best: reference *Otherworld*.

"Hey."

She grins. "Yeah?"

"Remember the episode where Baskerville sees the UFO, and runs to tell Gemma?" I ask.

"And then it disappears as soon as she shows up?" Cat says. "Yes. That was so infuriating."

"What if we stay here all night, and then I go to . . . I don't know, throw our burrito wrappers away or something. And you see one again—but then it vanishes the second I get back? Same-same."

"I'm sorry, are you Gemma Monroe in this scenario?" she teases.

"Hey, I'd be *happy* to be Gemma Monroe. I'd also love to be her soulmate and husband. It's all good."

Cat swats at me playfully. "Ha, ha. Well, I'll just have to be the one to leave. Then both of us will have seen a UFO."

We both lie back down, and silence spreads between us like a black hole. Suddenly, it feels like this whole moment could die if I don't speak. But, before I can open my mouth, Cat is the one to break it.

"Sam?"

"Yeah?"

"Thank you for believing me."

My stomach flutters in a way that is *not* burrito-related. "Ummm, thank you for not being a total jerk."

"What?"

"It's a better compliment than you think! You reminded me that people can be . . . good."

"Mmm," she says. Then, she lays her hand down flat, palm up.

I stare at it like it's a nuclear weapon. What should I do? Should I hold her hand? Is she going to hold mine? Wait . . . is my hand even available? I pull both out from behind me and just stare at them. Sweet Diddy of *Kong,* why am I so bad at this?

Cat laughs. "Hold my hand, dork!"

Maybe *this* is the best moment ever. I reach out and lace my fingers through hers. It's a *real* hand-hold. Not that one-on-top-of-the-other stuff from the other day. Nobody can pretend we're not holding hands right now.

This is not a drill. I repeat, *not* a drill.

But, as I squeeze Cat's hand, I notice something else. Once my racing heartbeat starts to slow, I realize that a crush isn't the only thing happening right now. Even though Cat is definitely *not* Oscar, the way this feels isn't so different from sitting on his bed—playing video games and laughing way too hard. I feel . . . safe.

And very much *not* alone.

I close my eyes, wondering if this is all a dream. Then, the inky-black darkness behind my eyelids lightens and turns red, then yellow-orange.

"Sam!" Cat cries.

My eyes fly open, and we both stare into the brilliant beam of light.

✶ AUTHOR'S NOTE ✶

I've been telling everyone that this story was twelve years in the making. But, in a real way, this has been in my head and my heart for the past thirty.

A month from my writing this author's note will mark thirty years since my best friend, Jamin, died less than a year after being diagnosed with Hodgkin's lymphoma. I'd known her since infancy—often thinking of her more as a sister than a friend. I was an odd kid with so many social strikes against me, but Jamin never made me feel that way. She enthusiastically starred in the murder-mystery skits I wrote from scratch. She hid under the table with me at parties to eat cake and spy on our parents. She shared in my wild imagination, and *always* made me laugh.

When Jamin died, a part of me clung to her existence

in this world so fiercely that I wondered if fate made the right choice taking her instead of me. What a horrible thought for a thirteen-year-old to have—but I had it. Like Sam did with Oscar, I tried to hear Jamin after she passed. I even wrote notes to myself in her handwriting, pretending that she was still somehow communicating with me. I spent that entire school year imagining that there would be a phone call and it would be the hospital, calling to let us know that it was all some big mistake. Getting through that time felt impossible. But I did get through it.

Then, years later in 2011, I got another call—*I* had cancer. Like Sam, it was mostly "good" news on the balance. I would have to have two surgeries, radiation therapy, and a decade of treatment, but I would (likely) live. But that news didn't sink in until I had a few years cancer-free under my belt—and there are still days I'm not quite sure. In this book, Sam thinks of cancer a little like the monster in a scary movie. It always feels as if it's just around the corner, waiting for you. Sometimes the fear can be worse than the disease.

After getting my diagnosis, I acted like the true librarian I am: I read everything I could get my hands on. I even went back and read an old Sweet Valley High book featuring a character with cancer. That was . . . not a good choice. The issue was that everything I read made me *more* scared. People often see cancer as one of two extremes: either you have cancer and should be afraid, or you don't have it and everything is fine. The truth, like most things, is much more nuanced. Living with cancer puts you in a strange in-between place, like the one Sam inhabits. You're not a one-person inspirational throw pillow, or a fierce warrior. You're just a person who wants to get better.

So often, I see illness and disability focused on a character "overcoming" it. It's a message laced with the best intentions: to bring hope to someone who is struggling. But it can have the opposite impact, instead causing real harm and making people feel like the "other" by framing their story as inspiration for those who *aren't* struggling. This is why Sam's story has a lot of negative self-talk—while it's hard to see, it reflects my experience fighting against that expectation of "overcoming." If you are a reader living with chronic illness or disability, I especially want to speak to *you* with this story and say this:

Being strong can look a lot like watching television or playing video games on the couch. No magical sword needed! Also, an illness getting worse doesn't make you weak—and it doesn't mean you failed. You have every right to feel angry or sad about it sometimes. But you also get to feel proud of yourself. Those feelings—good and bad—are yours to have because this is *your* experience.

If you think differently than other people (like I did, and do), please know that who you are is valuable—no "overcoming" necessary. Neurodiversity is just that—*diversity*. It can add necessary color to the canvas that is this world. Your uniqueness helps you see the world in a way that's both needed and awesome. Don't let anyone tell you otherwise.

My late father-in-law, Joel, said something that has always stuck with me. He said that "life is lumpy." There will be periods that are rough and smooth for *everyone* in the course of their lives. With that in mind, I also dearly hope for one last thing for you, readers. I hope that Sam and Cat remind those of you going through your own Big Things™ that hard times can have good times too. You're allowed to smile, and laugh, and even feel joy in some of those moments if it helps you through. Because those momentary and beautiful glimmers can guide us through even the darkest of times.

✶ ACKNOWLEDGMENTS ✶

So many people played a role in bringing this book into the world.

To my agent, the irreplaceable Chelsea Eberly: with every book, I am more grateful for you. Between the orca-strong advocacy, emotional support, and editing prowess, I remain shocked that I was lucky enough to get an agent like you. A HUGE thanks to The Rights People as well for bringing my book to the world, and to the whole Greenhouse team.

To my amazing editor, Emilia—thanks so much for giving me the space to create a character and story with this much nuance. I know not every editor would give me that freedom and I'll be eternally grateful! I owe so much to the whole Harper team (Briana, Sammy, and so many more!) for your parts in bringing Sam's story to life. A huge shout-out to Elena Stokes, Tanya Farrell, and the whole Wunderkind team for your publicity work— I'm so lucky to have you all! Thanks, too, to my cover artist Alisha Monnin, for your absolutely gorgeous work and attention to the details of the story.

Several bookish people also offered support and insight for this book, and for my books in general. Much appreciation to Joe McGee for your thoughtful insights into Sam's journey. Imagine me saying "and my axe!" in the fellowship to take down cancer. Thanks to the incredible Lauren Magaziner for your kind words about my work, and for giving me real truths, with a spoonful of sugar, about what might come in this process. I want to shout out Becky Albertalli, who gave me the confidence (and the context) to enter the queer lit space despite having imposter syndrome. I'll be eternally grateful that you extended your friendship to a baby bi like myself. I also want to express my gratitude to Books, Inc. (and especially the phenomenal Colleen Cadiz!) for being so welcoming, uplifting my work, and being a safe space for a new author when bookstores became scary for me.

I will *always* thank teachers and librarians to the moon and back! Teachers are quite literally risking it all to keep our kids safe and uplift them for who they are—you deserve *so* much more than you get and I won't be satisfied until you're pulling pro-ballplayer money. Librarians, too, have long been fighting another epidemic in this country: book banning and the attempted erasure of queer and BIPOC stories. Thank you. You have made me brave enough to keep telling my stories even though it's scary at times.

With each book, I like to give thanks to those who provided much-needed inspiration. Thanks to the creators, actors, and crew of the *X-Files* for inspiring *Otherworld* to the point where I now want it to exist on its own. To Jenny and Kristin of Buffering's *The E(eeeee) x-Files* for immersing me in the fandom and inspiring me all over again. Lastly, I need to nerdfighter out and thank John and Hank Green. John, you inspired me to write my own cancer story after I read *TFIOS*. Hank, you made honest, educational, and hilarious videos during your cancer journey that I both wish I had twelve years ago and *know* so many will benefit from today.

I will never, ever forget the medical professionals who helped me in the months after my diagnosis. Thanks to Dr. Stuntz for telling me I was probably going to live right off the bat—and also for being a surgeon so precise that doctors *still* tell me they can't see the scars. I will be eternally grateful to my radiation oncologist, Dr. Feehan, who looked me right in the face the first time he met me, glanced at my chart, and said "well, this *sucks*." I'm here today and have a beautiful daughter because of both of you.

Writers live in a vacuum without critique. So, this next one goes out to my steadfast critique reader besties. I would have crumbled and imploded into dust without the help of (debut author of the highly anticipated YA novel *I Wish You Would*!) Eva Des Lauriers. You are my CP, my podcast partner (*Write Where It Hurts*), and my friend. And then there's my longtime best friend/brother/soul twin and talented editor, Karim, who has worked on *every* one of my books and somehow continues to do so even though it takes a massive amount of time? Thank you seems too little, but I'll say it anyway: I am so grateful and lucky to have you both in my corner.

To my dear friend Jamin—and Steve, Pril, and Sam!—so much love to you always. To my extended family and my friends (you know who you are!), your support through all of this was everything to me. Thanks to my mom-in-law, Melly, and to Joel for "life is lumpy." It is!

Thanks to my mom, who stayed up late after teaching all day to edit my first novel—and to my dad, who shouted about my writing from the rooftops every chance he could get. I would *never* have had the confidence to write if it weren't for both of you (possibly unreasonably) inflating my ego about my writing talent. All books are in some way written for my sister, Maren. The book blogger. The webmaster. The legend. I *live* to make you laugh. Torso.

These books would not happen if it were not for the time carved out by my husband and soul mate, Ben. But this book in particular owes you a lot. I wanted to write a boy character raised in a culinarily Jewish family, and you helped me make sure the details were right on both fronts. To my daughter, Mia, who (at only eight!) gave me the best writing advice I'll ever get: *"write your book your own way."* I wrote this book because I wanted you to see a family that looked like ours. I hope you like it.

And, finally, to all the kids who don't quite fit into a box—this is for you.